THE ANIMAL RESCUE SQUAD™

#2

Hand-Me-Down Chimp

by Ellen Weiss
and Mel Friedman

BULLSEYE BOOKS

Random House ⌂ New York

For Nora, saver of strays.

*The authors would like to thank
Dr. Herb Terrace of Columbia University
and, most of all, Nim Chimpsky.*

Reprinted by arrangement with Random House, Inc.
10   9   8   7   6   5   4   3   2   1

A BULLSEYE BOOK PUBLISHED BY RANDOM HOUSE, INC.

Library of Congress Catalog Card Number: 94-72276
ISBN: 0-679-85866-0
RL: 3.2

First Bullseye Books edition: June 1995

Manufactured in the United States of America

THE ANIMAL RESCUE SQUAD is a trademark of Random House, Inc.

Contents

My Big Chance

If you're going to understand anything about this story, there are some things you should know about me right away. So I guess I'll just tell you.

My name is Lisa Ho, and I'm crazy about animals. (Some people say I'm crazy, period, but *I* think I'm perfectly sane.) I love all animals, except maybe giant five-foot Australian worms, and this is why I'm a member of the Animal Rescue Squad. There are four of us in the Animal Rescue Squad: me, my best friend Eliza Spain, Molly Penrose, and Abby Goodman. We all love animals to smithereens, and we do anything we can to help them. My own particular thing is apes, ever since I saw *Gorillas in the Mist*, this movie about a scientist who studies gorillas in the jungle, and her favorite gorilla gets killed by hunters, and I cried my eyes out for three days. The movie made me feel that apes are so much smarter and more dignified than people. After I saw it, I plastered my room with pictures of gorillas.

Anyway, our story opens, as so many do, with a phone call. Actually, it was two phone calls. I was talking to Eliza about all the Animal Rescue Squad's plans for the summer when I heard a short beep in my ear, telling me I had another call coming in. "Hold on," I said to her. "Call waiting." I pushed the button on the phone.

"Hello?" I said, fanning myself with a magazine. It was one of those end-of-June days that feels like the middle of August.

"Hi, Lisa, it's Tom." Tom is my cousin. He's in college, studying philosophy or something.

"Oh, hi, Tom," I began. "I'm just on—"

"Lisa, I have this huge problem," he said at the same time. "I have to find somebody who can take care of this chimp for a week. It's kind of an emergency. I thought your parents might know somebody—"

Somebody to take care of a chimp! This was the most thrilling thing I had ever heard in my life!

"Wait, hold on a second, Tom," I interrupted. "I'm on the other line. I'll get back to you in a second."

"Oh, sorry," he said.

"Be right back," I said. I clicked the button again. "Eliza!" I said. "You'll never guess what!"

"What?"

"My cousin Tom is on the other line. You know, the one in college? He has to find somebody to take care of a *chimp* for a week!"

"Wow!" she said.

"Hold on a second," I said. "I'm going back to him."

I clicked the button again. "Tom? Are you there?"

"Where else would I be?"

"So, tell me about this chimp." I was trying to sound calm, but I wasn't. I already knew I wanted this chimp more than I'd ever wanted anything.

"I don't know a lot about it. Apparently he was part of some kind of big experiment. My friend Jane was working on it. She's studying psychology. So, now the experiment's over, and Jane was supposed to take care of the chimp this week, until the zoo he's going to finishes building a special area for him. But the problem is, Jane got into a bad car accident last night."

"Yikes—is she going to be okay?"

"Eventually. She broke both legs and some bones in her hand. But she called me from the hospital, with practically her last breath, and asked me to help with the chimp. I've only had him for a night and he's already destroying my dorm room. I haven't been able to get any studying done, and I'm sure they'll kick me out if they find out he's here. I need help, fast. I've called everybody I know—I've even called people I *don't* know."

I had already made my mind up. My heart was thumping. "Hold on," I said. "I'll be right back."

I clicked back to Eliza.

"Eliza!" I said. "Guess what?"

"No, I'm scared to," she said.

"I'm going to take this chimp for a week!"

Eliza let out a scream. "Unbelievable!" she cried. Then she sobered up. "But how are you going to get your parents to let you?"

"Well, I have to ask them. But I'm sure I can get them to say yes. I'm *meant* to do this," I said. "It's the chance of my lifetime!"

"I know, I know. It's the chance of the Rescue Squad's lifetime!"

"Hold on, I have to go back to Tom." I clicked again. "Tom," I said, "I've decided. I'm going to take the chimp."

There was a long silence. "Lisa," he said finally, "that's ridiculous. You're only a kid."

"I'm *eleven*. And I know a lot about animals," I said. "I'm a member of the Animal Rescue Squad, you know. We rescue animals all the time. Between us we've rescued four dogs, a cat, a baby raccoon, and a whole animal shelter."

"You know I'd love to unload him right this second, but this is crazy. What are your parents going to say?"

"I'll work it out. Trust me."

"I don't know—"

"Just let me call my parents. Then I'll call you right back."

"Okay," he said uncertainly.

"Okay, 'bye," I said before he could change his mind.

I clicked to Eliza. "I'm so excited!" I shrieked. "I'm going to take the chimp!"

"Lisa," said Eliza, "I've been thinking while I've been waiting. I'm not sure if the Animal Rescue Squad can handle this. It really might be too much." I could just see her pushing her thick glasses up on her nose, the way she always did when she was worrying. Her frizzy hair seemed to frizz up more when she worried, too. She worried a lot.

"*I* can handle it. I gotta call my parents," I said. "I'll call you back later."

In another minute I was on the phone with the nurse at my parents' medical clinic. Since we're Chinese-American, my parents do both Chinese and Western medicine—everything from acupuncture to penicillin.

"Hi, Mei-Ling," I said. "Are my parents available?"

"Well, your mother is just about to take a patient. Maybe she could talk to you for a minute."

Perfect, I thought. I could usually talk my mother into things that my father wouldn't hear of.

She came to the phone. "Hi, honey, is anything wrong?" she asked.

"No, nothing's wrong. It's just that—well, I have to ask you something."

I told her about Tom's call. "He's desperate," I said. "He needs somebody to help him, right now. I know I can do this. It's just for a week. I'll keep him in my room. You won't even know he's there." Then I hit her with the line I knew would work best: "Mom, it's *science*. Think how much I'll *learn* if I do this." My parents are suckers for learning, especially science. They've always let me do anything I wanted, including having a colony of red ants in my room, as long as I was learning.

"I don't know," she said. "It's a big responsibility…"

"Please?" I begged. "I'm sure Eliza's mother will help me." Eliza's mother is a veterinarian.

"I need to talk to your father about this. I can't decide to have a chimp in the house without talking to him. I'll call you back in half an hour."

"Okay," I said dejectedly.

As long as I had to wait, I decided to use the time. First I went to the bookcase and took out volume 3 of the encyclopedia. I turned to "Chimpanzee," settling down on the sofa with an apple.

"Chimpanzee," I read to myself. "A tailless anthropoid (manlike) ape, not to be confused with a monkey…Robust, outgoing, and lively…Like humans, has an opposable thumb and flat fingernails…Known for its intelligence and trainability…Can learn human forms of communication…Active during the day, usually sleeps at night in a nest it builds in a tree…Mainly vegetarian diet, eats fruits, vegetables, seeds…Termites, ants, and sometimes meat are also eaten…Can grow to be five feet tall and weigh 175 pounds…"

Holy cow! Five feet tall and 175 pounds! I'd thought they were kind of cute, cuddly little toddler-sized guys. What if it was taller than me and three times as heavy? What if it wasn't *toilet trained*?

I threw down the encyclopedia and ran into the kitchen, grabbing the address book on the way to the phone. Flipping madly to the "Ho" page, I scanned the lines until I found Tom's number. I dialed it fast.

"Tom?" I said as soon as he answered. "How big is it? Is it toilet trained? Is it a huge monster?"

He laughed. "I guess this is Lisa, huh?"

I giggled. "Sorry," I said. "Yeah, this is me. I just got a little scared reading the encyclopedia."

"Okay, here's all I know about him. His name is Gumbo. He's really friendly. He *is* toilet trained—he kind of grabs your shirt and pulls you toward the bathroom when he has to go. He's not huge, he doesn't even come up to my waist. I think he's about two. He's very cute, you just have to watch him every second."

"Whew," I said. "Thank goodness."

"What did your parents say? No, right?"

"My mother has to talk to my father. She's going to call me in a few minutes."

"Okay. Call me when they call you."

I had one more phone call I needed to make. I flipped through the address book again until I found the number for Eliza's mother's office.

Eloise the receptionist knows me well, because I sometimes go over there with Eliza to help out with jobs like feeding the animals and cleaning the cages. "Hi, Lisa," she said. "I think Dr. Spain can talk to you now."

Eliza's mother is really nice. I explained the chimp problem to her and asked if she could help me.

I could hear her take a deep breath. "You don't know what you're getting yourself into," she said.

"It's only for a week," I said. "School's over, so I have nothing to do but take care of the chimp. I'll work really hard. I can do it, I know I can."

"Well, if your parents say yes, which I'm sure they won't, I'll help you as much as I can. I'm no expert on chimps, though. I didn't take the ape course in veterinary school. But I think I know somebody who knows a lot. I just have to remember who it is."

I whooped with joy. "Thank you, thank you, thank you!" I said. "I know I can handle this."

"All right, let me know what happens."

I thanked her again, said good-bye, and put down the phone feeling much better about the whole thing.

I heard the soft padding of feet coming down the stairs. It was my grandmother, a tiny little lady with gray hair in a tight bun. She always wears a black sweater that buttons up the front, even in summer. Sometimes people don't take her seriously, because she's four feet tall. But when she gets mad, she has the temper of a dragon.

"Hi, *Nainai*," I said in Chinese. She doesn't speak any English. "Have you been taking a nap?"

"Yes, and now I'm going to have some tea," she said. "Would you like some?"

"No, thanks." I pondered whether I should mention the chimp to her. I decided not to. Something told me she would not love the idea.

While she was putting up the water for her tea, the phone rang. It was my mother.

"Well, I've spoken to your father," she said. "Neither of us is crazy about this idea."

My heart sank.

"We're at least willing to entertain the possibility," she said, "but we have a few questions."

My heart soared. "Ask away," I said.

"We need to find out how big this animal is, what it eats, whether it's toilet trained, and whether Eliza's mother really will help you out."

I breathed a big sigh of relief. "As a matter of fact," I said, "I know the answers to all those questions." I told her about my conversation with Tom, my encyclopedia reading, and my talk with Dr. Spain.

"Well, I must say," said my mother, "I'm impressed with how responsible you're being. You've really tried to find out as much as you could."

"Yup," I said modestly.

"Okay. I guess we can let you try it. But he stays in your room. You are not to drive your grandmother crazy with this. If there's any trouble, he goes right back to your cousin. Tom will have to figure out something else."

"Yay!" I yelled. "You are the greatest mother in the whole wide world!"

"Just make sure you keep him out of everybody's hair. This is your job, and only yours."

"I will! I promise!" I hollered. "I totally swear!"

"I've got to see a patient now. You can call

Tom and tell him to drive the chimp up here tomorrow morning."

I said good-bye to her and jumped up and down for about five minutes. I couldn't believe the incredible thing that was about to happen to me.

Then I sat my grandmother down and tried to explain to her about who was coming to stay at our house.

Enter Gumbo

At eight o'clock the next morning, Saturday, the doorbell rang. I had been up for hours. I pounded down the stairs and looked out the little window in the door. There was Tom— and there was Gumbo.

Tom was carrying the chimp on his hip, just like a toddler. Gumbo was the cutest thing I had ever seen in my life. You could tell he was a little-kid chimp, because he *looked* like a little kid. He was wearing little blue-and-white striped overalls and a red T-shirt.

When I flung open the door, Gumbo hung back, looking shy. He buried his face in Tom's collar and made soft whimpering noises.

I couldn't take my eyes off him. I had never been near a monkey or ape before, and I didn't really understand how they worked. I knew he wasn't a child, but he wasn't a dog or a cat either. What would it be like taking care of him? I was beginning to feel a little nervous.

Gumbo was obviously nervous too, and wouldn't stop clinging to Tom. I knew from baby-sitting that when little kids are shy, the best thing to do is pretty much ignore them until they get used to you, and then they'll come to you on their own. I decided that until I figured out what I was dealing with, I'd just pretend Gumbo was a little kid. I talked to Tom instead of making a big fuss over Gumbo.

"You're so early!" I said. I knew that it was about a two-hour drive from the university in Boston to our town—we're off the coast—so we hadn't expected Tom until at least about ten. My parents were still sleeping.

"Gumbo's an early riser," said Tom, looking exhausted. "I figured I might as well pack him up and get going." He handed me a small suitcase. "His clothes are in here," he said.

I was kind of surprised that Gumbo wore clothes. "What kind of an experiment was he in, anyway?" I asked.

"I have no idea," he replied. "Jane was too groggy to tell me much of anything."

I put the suitcase at the foot of the stairs. "How was the ride up?" I asked.

"Well, he's obviously been for rides in the car before. He seemed used to it. I had to strap him into his seat in the back, though. When we tried the front, he drove me nuts pushing all the buttons and turning the knobs. Luckily, this stuff kept him busy for most of the ride." He held up a net bag, inside which I could see some board books and stuffed animals.

"Those are very nice toys," I said, making a big show of inspecting them. "I have some toys for Gumbo, too." I actually didn't have any toys for Gumbo, because I hadn't known what he'd be like. But I was starting to figure it out very fast. He had the most expressive face, with deep and intelligent eyes.

I ran into the kitchen and grabbed a set of red plastic measuring cups that nested together. Little kids who visited us always liked to play with them.

Tom came in and sat down on the sofa, still holding Gumbo. I sat down beside them and offered the measuring cups to Gumbo. He looked away and drew back his lips in a sort of smile.

"Here," I said. "You can play with them. It's okay."

Very gingerly, he reached out a wrinkly hand and touched the cups with one finger. He was definitely interested in them. I stared at his hand. I couldn't believe how almost-human it looked. Gumbo's hand made it really clear what "opposable thumb" meant: He could grab something between his thumb and another finger the way a person could. I thought about how hard it would be to get anything accomplished without an opposable thumb.

I offered the cups again. "They're cups," I said. "Fun to play with." This time, Gumbo decided to go for it. He reached for them and snatched them out of my hand. He put them down on the sofa in front of him and separated them, lining them up in a row. Then he put them back together, trying them out until he figured out which ones went inside which. For some reason, he made a strange hand movement before he picked up each cup.

"Good going, Gumbo!" I said. "You figured out how to put them together!" I clapped for him, and he clapped his hands, too, making small ooh-ooh-ooh noises. I was already falling in love.

"Now, I don't know a lot about taking care of him," said Tom, "but I'll tell you what I know. You can feed him practically anything you could feed a person. He eats pretty often. If you want to walk him outside, you can use the belt thing with the leash attached that's in his suitcase. I can't tell you where to put him to sleep—he slept with me both nights, and it wasn't too comfortable for either of us."

"I'll figure something out," I said.

Tom stood up. "Well," he said, "gotta go. I have a class at eleven."

I was startled. "Don't you even want to stay to—" I began.

"Nope, gotta go. Say hi to your parents for me." He took Gumbo's hand and shook it. "'Bye, pal," he said. "It's been nice knowing you. Sort of nice."

An alarmed look passed over Gumbo's face. As Tom walked to the door, Gumbo hopped off the sofa and followed him, trailing his knuckles on the floor and making a soft hooting noise.

"Sorry, Gumbo, you can't come with me. You're going to stay here with Lisa for a week. She's very nice, you'll see." Tom opened the door, and Gumbo attached himself to his leg, looking panic-stricken. "Oh, rats," muttered Tom. "Now what do I do?"

I had an idea. Running into the kitchen, I grabbed a banana from the bowl on the counter and ran back to the door with it.

"Look, Gumbo," I said. "Look what I have. A nice banana for you."

Gumbo looked interested. He loosened his grip on Tom's leg a bit.

"C'mon over here and I'll give it to you," I said. "Mmmm, it's so good." I started to peel it.

That did it. Gumbo let go of Tom and headed for the banana. I picked him up and let him help me peel the banana the rest of the way. He felt nice in my arms, solid but not too heavy. His fur was thick, but surprisingly soft. He had a scent that I had never smelled before, kind of musky. It was actually nice. Gumbo took a bite of the banana as Tom eased out the door.

"'Bye," Tom said softly to me. "And thanks!" Just before he closed the door, he opened it again. "Almost forgot," he said. "Here are some papers that came with him. And I have a couple of phone numbers for you. Here's the number of the zoo Gumbo's going to, so they can figure out how to get him from you. And here's my friend Jane's number in the hospital. But please try not to bother her. She needs to get better without worrying."

"Okay," I said.

Tom closed the door, and Gumbo and I were alone.

"So," I said. "What do you want to do?"

Gumbo just kept looking at the door, where Tom had been, and whimpering.

"I have an idea," I said. "Let's go sit on the sofa and read a book. Would you like that?"

Gumbo kept looking at the door.

I carried him over to the sofa and sat him down beside me. Grabbing the net bag Tom had brought along, I pulled out the books that were inside.

"Oh, look!" I said with exaggerated excitement. "Here's a book about getting dressed! Look, Gumbo, here's Baby Bear getting dressed. He's putting on his shirt. See his shirt?" I pointed to the picture. "Do you have a shirt, too?"

Gumbo couldn't keep himself from getting interested in the book. He climbed into my lap and scrutinized the picture.

"Baby Bear has a nice red shirt, just like you," I pointed out. Gumbo plucked happily at his shirt, and pointed at the shirt in the picture. Then he held his hand in front of his chest, palm up, and flipped it over. Then he plucked at his shirt and flipped his hand over again. It was the second time I had seen him make strange hand movements, and I wondered why he did it. I obviously had a lot to learn about chimpanzees and their odd little habits.

I turned the page. "Oh, look at that!" I said in amazement. "He has pants on now!" I pointed to Baby Bear's pants. "You have overalls on, Gumbo," I said, "don't you?"

Gumbo made a motion that looked a lot like pulling pants up. It was really something. What a smart little guy he was!

On the stairs I heard the sound of tiny feet descending. It was the moment of truth: My grandmother was up. I decided to keep things very cool. I didn't get up, just kept pointing out the picture to Gumbo. Maybe this wouldn't be too bad. She reached the bottom of the stairs.

"Aiieee!" shrieked my grandmother. "A monkey! There's a monkey in the house!"

Gumbo freaked out. He scrambled out of my lap, leaped to the end of the sofa, grabbed the drapes hanging beside the window, climbed them to the top, and hung there, screeching. Now they were both screeching, Gumbo and my grandmother.

"He's not a monkey, *Nainai*, he's a chimpanzee. And I told you he was coming, remember? Now look, you've scared him."

"It's an animal! It's a wild animal!" she yelled. She kept going on like this as I approached Gumbo carefully and tried to talk him into getting down from the drapes. Between Gumbo and my grandmother, the racket was awful.

My mother appeared on the stairs behind my grandmother. "What's happening?" she asked, rubbing her eyes. Then she saw Gumbo. "Oh, my God," she said. "It's here."

"Everything was fine," I shouted over the din. "He was really being good until *Nainai* started screaming at him. If I can get some peace and quiet with him, I know I can get him calmed down."

My mother put her arm around my grandmother's shoulder. "Let's just go back upstairs and pretend this never happened," she said in Chinese. "Later, we can come down and everything will be better. Lisa will keep the chimp in her room." She shot me a look. "Won't you, Lisa?"

"Yes, I promise," I said. "He just got here, for heaven's sake. If you just give him a chance, you'll like him a lot. He's really cute."

"Maybe later," said my mother. "Right now, I'm taking your grandmother back upstairs. When we come down for breakfast

21

in a little while, you'll have him in your room, right?"

"Right," I said.

My mother helped my grandmother back up the stairs. My grandmother had stopped screaming and was merely muttering to herself about "that ugly monkey."

"Sorry to surprise you, *Nainai*," I called after her.

Gumbo had quieted down a bit as the situation got less hysterical. He was still clinging to the drapes, though. For the first time, I noticed his feet. They looked almost exactly like human hands, even more than his hands did. He was holding on to the curtains with them.

"You can come down now, Gumbo," I coaxed him. "It's safe. Nobody will hurt you."

He just looked at me mistrustfully.

I ran into the kitchen again and this time emerged with four Oreos. "Look," I said. "Cookies. You can have them if you come down."

He looked interested, but still didn't move.

I took a little bite of one. "Mmmm," I said "These are the best cookies I ever tasted. Chocolate on the outside, white stuff on the inside. See?"

22

He stretched out his hand for one, but couldn't reach it. I moved away a little, so he'd have to come down. "Yummy yummy," I said, having another nibble.

Nervously glancing toward the stairs, Gumbo finally decided to make his move. He clambered back down the curtains and made a snatch for the cookies in my hand.

"Ah-ah-ah," I said. "You have to be polite." I sat down on the sofa, and he sat down beside me. "Now," I said, "would you like a cookie, Gumbo?" I offered him one slowly, and he took it gently from my hand.

"Very good!" I said. "Good Gumbo." He scarfed down his cookie. "Now," I said, "I'm going to teach you the *right* way to eat an Oreo. Watch carefully."

I put his Oreo into my lap and screwed mine apart. Then I licked off the white stuff. "See?" I said. "That's how you're supposed to do it."

I handed Gumbo his Oreo. "Take it apart, Gumbo," I said. "Just the way I did." He started lifting it to his mouth. "No, take it apart," I said. He regarded the Oreo intently, and then he screwed it apart.

"Yay!" I said. "Good Gumbo! Now lick off the inside!"

He did, smacking his lips a whole lot.

Then he gobbled the rest of the cookie.

"You are so smart!" I clapped. Gumbo bounced up and down on the sofa, grunting.

"Okay." I started to get up. "Now we have to go upstairs to my room. We're going to be spending most of our time up there, okay?" He stared at me. "C'mon," I said, holding my arms out. He stared at me some more. I squatted down next to him. "Want a piggyback ride?" I said, holding my arms out behind me this time.

Gumbo hopped on, holding on around my neck. He seemed to be used to doing this. I grabbed his suitcase and his net bag full of toys and books, and trudged up to my room on the third floor with him. It was lucky we'd have a whole floor to ourselves—my room and a bathroom were the only rooms up there. Maybe I could keep him out of the way.

I sat down on my bed, huffing and puffing, and let Gumbo off. Then I mopped my forehead. "Boy, Gumbo," I said, "it sure is hot and you sure are heavy." But Gumbo was already inspecting his new surroundings. He picked up everything on my night table—my pen, my diary, my lamp, my roll of Life Savers, and my flashlight—and inspected them carefully, one by one. Some of them he tested with his mouth. I held my breath until he was finished, hoping he wouldn't decide to eat anything.

Then he hopped off the bed and trundled over to my chest of drawers. The bottom drawer was open. He pulled out a bathing suit bottom, looked at it with great interest, and then put it on his head.

"That's not a hat, Gumbo." I laughed, taking it off him.

I bent down to put the bathing suit back in the drawer, and when I straightened up, I noticed he was pulling at my sweatshirt.

"What's the matter, Gumbo?" I asked.

He kept pulling. "What is it, little guy?" I was puzzled. Then I realized he was trying to pull me toward the door of my room.

I remembered what Tom had said about the bathroom. Could that be it? I decided to let Gumbo pull me for a little way, and see what happened.

Sure enough, we headed for the bathroom. He must have seen it when we came up the stairs. Gumbo stood by the toilet. I stood by Gumbo. Then I figured out what the problem was. "Can't you undo your overalls?" I asked him, bending down and fiddling with the fasteners.

Once I'd gotten his overalls down, he knew just what to do. He even knew what to do with the toilet paper. It was great. Then he hopped off, flushed, and waited for me to do up his overalls again. "Good boy, Gumbo!" I crowed. "This isn't going to be so hard!" He threw his arms around me and I picked him up and carried him happily into my room.

The phone rang and I picked up the extension next to my bed. It was Abby. "Lisa!" she yelled. "Is it true? You have a *chimp* in your house?"

"He's right here in my room with me," I said. "Abby, he's so cute you'll *die*. But he's really hard to take care of. You have to help me."

"Of course we'll help you. Can you bring him to the Rescue Squad meeting at Eliza's house tomorrow?"

I had forgotten about the meeting. "Sure!" I said. "That would be great!"

"I have to go to practice now. I just wanted to see if it was true." Abby's seriously into gymnastics. She has to practice for hours every day.

"Okay," I said. "I'll see you tomorrow."

There was a knock on my door. It was both my parents. "Come on in and meet Gumbo," I said.

Gumbo was sitting on my bed and coloring on a large sketch pad, making a big scribble with red and blue crayons. He looked up as they nervously entered the room.

"See?" I said. "He's nice. He's a lot like a little kid."

"I want you to know, Lisa," said my father, "that I'm not convinced this is a good idea. Your mother had to talk me into letting you try it. But I don't want your grandmother upset, and I won't have our house turned upside-down by this animal."

"Yes, Dad," I said earnestly. "I really understand. I'm going to be *so* careful. But could you do me a favor?"

"What is it?"

"Maybe you could bring *Nainai* in here, really carefully, so she can see him in a calmer way. I know she won't be scared of him if she's prepared. Look how cute he is."

My dad seemed unmoved by Gumbo's adorableness, but he agreed. He went downstairs to get her, and my mother sat down on the bed, near Gumbo (but not too near). He gave her a big grin.

"Thanks for talking Dad into this, Mom," I said.

"Nice picture, Gumbo," said my mother.

A minute later, my father reappeared with my grandmother in tow. This time, she seemed a bit calmer about the whole thing.

She edged into the room, not taking her eyes off Gumbo. He eyed her warily.

"He's smart?" she asked me.

"Very smart," I replied.

"Smarter than a dog?"

"Much smarter."

"But not as smart as a person," she said.

"Almost. Almost as smart as a small child."

"He doesn't bite, does he?" she asked.

"I don't think so," I said.

Gumbo made a final flourish in gold crayon on his picture, hopped off the bed, and presented it to my grandmother. She was still trying to look severe, but I could see a smile trying to turn up the corners of her mouth.

Things were going to be okay.

Gumbo Meets Little, Big, and Archie

I spent the rest of the day in my room with Gumbo, looking for ways to keep him busy. I couldn't very well leave him in my room alone at lunchtime, so I got permission from my parents to bring him to the table. His manners were pretty good except for a tendency to smack his lips loudly, but at least he didn't grab things. He could even use a spoon and a fork. He seemed to like grapes and broccoli best, but he had a good time with the spaghetti, too. "Sorry, pal," I said. "We don't have any termites for you. Tuna fish will have to do."

My grandmother still didn't feel completely comfortable with him, but I did notice that every now and then she'd slip him a grape.

That evening, I asked my dad if he'd come

upstairs and help me put up my old hammock. He'd strung it across my room for me when I was six and I'd announced to him that I was going to sleep in a hammock for the rest of my life. That idea had only lasted about three weeks, but we still had the hammock. I figured it would be good for Gumbo, since he was supposed to sleep in a nest in the trees.

Gumbo watched my father very intently as he screwed the hooks into the door frame and the window frame and tested the hammock's strength. "Okay, Gumbo, hop in," said my dad, spreading it open for him.

With a screech of delight, Gumbo jumped into the hammock eagerly and lay down. He seemed made for it, and it for him.

"Well, that's that," said my father.

I pushed the hammock softly so it swayed a little. Gumbo made quiet, happy grunting noises. "I guess maybe it's bedtime," said my father. He kissed me on the forehead and tiptoed out of the room.

I helped Gumbo get undressed. Then I turned my lamp down low and sang him a lullaby, giving the hammock a little push now and then. His eyelids were getting heavy. As I sang, I remembered that one of the things in his net bag was a Raggedy Ann doll. Maybe he'd want to sleep with that. I took it out of the bag and he reached for it with both arms. Then he wrapped his long arms around my neck and pressed his face to mine. He lay back, snuggled Raggedy Ann's silly, smiling face right up to his, closed his eyes, and was out. I'd never had such a feeling of contentment in my life.

The next morning, I was awakened from a deep sleep by a gentle tapping on my nose. I dragged my eyes open and looked at my clock. Five-thirty.

"Oh, Gumbo," I said to him, batting him away as he tapped my nose with one finger. "Can't you go back to sleep for a while?"

He tapped harder.

I sat up. "Oh, all right. We'll get up." I rubbed my eyes. "But we have to be really quiet."

He pulled me to the bathroom, and our day began.

I got him dressed and carried him downstairs to scare up some breakfast. "Do you like cold cereal?" I asked him. "Or do you like oatmeal?" I wished he could talk. It would make everything so much easier.

I poured him a bowl of cornflakes and milk and sprinkled some raisins in. When I put it down in front of him, he made some

31

hand movements again, and then he picked out all the raisins, one by one, and lined them up on the edge of the table. Then he ate them.

"Well, I guess you like raisins, anyway."

I looked at the clock over the stove. It was 6:30 and we were all done with breakfast. What were we going to do with ourselves?

I decided that the quietest thing to do was to take him outside for a while. I had found the belt-and-leash thing in his suitcase, and I actually felt better knowing he wasn't going to be able to run away from me.

We went upstairs and got the leash, and he got really excited as I put it on him. I had to keep shushing him. I smuggled him out of the house as quietly as I could.

Closing the front door behind me, I realized that this was the earliest I had ever been outside in my life. The world was fresh and pretty at this hour. There was a wonderful strong smell blowing in from the ocean, which was only a few blocks away.

"Well, Gumbo, this is Dormouth, Massachusetts," I told him. "Let's go for a walk and look at your new neighborhood."

First I walked him past Molly's house. "This is Molly's house," I said, pointing to it. "She's in the Animal Rescue Squad. Molly and Abby and Eliza are going to help me take care of you, okay?"

We kept walking. I was glad there wasn't anybody out on the street yet. I didn't know if it would be okay to walk down the street with a chimpanzee. Maybe people would freak out. Maybe I'd even get arrested.

"This is Eliza's house," I said next. "She's my best, best friend. The meeting is going to be here."

Gumbo was having a fine old time. He seemed to love going for a walk, and he even liked stopping to smell the flowers. I kept the leash looped around my wrist, but I held his big, leathery hand just to be friendly.

We stopped at the playground behind the school. What a great idea that was! Gumbo climbed around the jungle gym with me trailing after him trying to keep the leash from getting tangled up. Then he swung his way across the overhead bars in about two seconds flat and went back and forth about fifty times, hooting and screeching. Watching him, I truly understood for the first time that he was a chimpanzee and not a little kid.

By the time we got home, we only had about an hour to kill before we'd have to leave for the Animal Rescue Squad meeting.

We went upstairs (this time I refused to carry Gumbo), went to the bathroom, and drew pictures together for a while. Then I said goodbye to my family and left. I couldn't wait to get to Eliza's with Gumbo.

It was the middle of the morning now so the streets weren't as deserted. Gumbo and I made quite a stir as we walked down the sidewalk. But nobody seemed scared of him, maybe because he was with me and on a leash. Everybody who passed either smiled or stopped to ask me questions about Gumbo. The Stiller sisters, Gertrude and Hortense, especially liked him. They're about ninety years old, and both sharp as tacks. "Look," said Gertrude to her sister, "he looks like that boyfriend you had—what was his name, Ernie?" "*Exactly* like Ernie!" cackled Hortense, and the two of them continued on down the street, laughing their heads off.

At ten o'clock sharp, Gumbo and I rang the bell at Eliza's big, rambling old house. (Actually, I let Gumbo ring the bell. He really wanted to push the button.)

Eliza threw open the door and shrieked. Gumbo buried his face in my neck, just the way he had snuggled into Tom's. I carried him into the living room. Abby and Molly

34

were already there, dying from curiosity and excitement.

I figured I'd better take charge as soon as I walked in. "No screaming," I ordered. "He'll just go nuts and climb the drapes. Just sort of play it cool until he gets used to the place, okay?"

"Okay," they all said at once.

"He's so cute I could die!" Abby whispered. Next to me, Abby Goodman is probably the most intense of the four of us. She's a champion gymnast, a horseback rider, and sometimes a model, but she still somehow manages to be a great person. She just kind of wades into situations and doesn't worry about getting messy. Once I was over being jealous of her I got to like her a lot.

Molly Penrose, the fourth member of the Animal Rescue Squad, looked a little less sure about Gumbo. When I plopped down on the sofa with him, she took a seat way over on the other side of the room. Molly is really special when you get to know her, but before you get to know her you might think she's kind of a fussbudget. She has to get everything just so before she's happy. She's into memorizing details about things. She has a very big heart, but I don't think she likes surprises too much. And if you don't like surprises, a chimpanzee just might not be your thing.

"Is he friendly?" she asked me.

Almost as if he had ESP or something, Gumbo threw his hairy arms around my neck and planted a noisy smack on my cheek.

"Very friendly," I said.

"We've got company," said Eliza.

Into the room trotted the Spain family's three dogs. Since Eliza loved animals maybe more than any of us, she was always picking up strays, and these three had stuck. There was a big, easygoing red one called Big, a little black one called Little who could sing, and a middle-sized scruffy brown one, a *very* bad troublemaker, named Archie. As soon as they spotted Gumbo, they edged over to inspect the new visitor.

It was hard to tell who was more nervous, Gumbo or the dogs. Gumbo pulled his lips back in a wide grin that I was beginning to realize meant he was anxious or scared. I figured I'd better deal with the situation, quick.

"Look, Gumbo—dogs," I said. "Nice dogs." I told all three of them to sit, and then I put my hand out and petted Big on the head. I figured he'd be the calmest. "Here, you can pet him, too."

I took Gumbo's hand and presented it to Big so he could sniff it. Then I showed Gumbo how to pat the dog's head. "Nice," I said. "Gentle."

Gumbo patted Big, who had his ears down uneasily but put up with it. "Thank you, Big," I said. "You're a good dog."

Gumbo had decided: He liked dogs. Bouncing up and down on the sofa, he petted Little next, so enthusiastically that I had to take his hand and remind him to be nice and gentle. When he tried to pet Archie, Archie ducked out from under his hand and went into his "play with me" crouch, with his front down and his behind in the air.

Gumbo got it right away. He bounced off the sofa and started chasing Archie, who ran into the dining room, yapping delightedly. "Uh-oh," said Eliza.

"I'll get him back," I said.

They tore around the house in a big circle, into the kitchen and back around to the living room, with me and Eliza chasing them. Gumbo was screeching happily, too. On this trip, they picked up Big and Little, and then all four of them went racing through the house. They ran up the stairs and back down in a flash, and once more around the dining room-kitchen-living room circuit.

Abby planted herself firmly in the middle of the living room and spread her arms out. "I've got him," she said. And sure enough, when Gumbo came tearing through the living room, he ran smack into Abby's arms, and she locked him in.

"Time to calm down," she said. She put Gumbo down on the sofa while Eliza made the dogs sit.

"It's a good thing my parents are both at work this morning," said Eliza.

"Well, everybody," I said, catching my breath, "this is Gumbo."

"How do you do, Gumbo?" said Abby, shaking hands with him.

Now that things were quieter, I could hear Eliza's big brother, Pete, playing his drums upstairs. Pete's in a band called the Screaming Mimis. He's thirteen, and I think he's the cutest boy I've ever seen. Eliza thinks I'm crazy, but that's because she's his sister. The problem is, he doesn't even know I'm alive, let alone what my name is.

Gumbo heard Pete's drums, too. He cocked his head, looking up toward the source of the sound. Then he scrambled off the sofa and made for the stairs.

"Let's let him go up," Eliza said. "It'll give Pete a good surprise."

"Are you sure?" I said.

"He's definitely heading for the sound of the drums. Look at him," said Eliza.

We all waited edgily as Gumbo disappeared up the stairs. A minute later, the sound of Pete's drums stopped. Then it started again.

"Let's go see," said Eliza.

We all jumped up and ran for the stairs. On the upstairs landing, we headed around to the left, toward Pete's room.

There was Gumbo, sitting on Pete's stool, playing the drums. He seemed to like the cymbal a lot, because he kept banging it, but he liked the drums, too. He was having a great time. Pete was standing beside him, shaking his head and grinning.

"This chimp is unreal," he said. "He plays the drums! Whose is he?"

"He's mine," I said. "Sort of."

Pete looked at me with new interest. There was a small explosion somewhere around my middle. "Cool," he said.

"I just have him for a week," I explained. "His name is Gumbo."

Gumbo hit the cymbal really hard. "Here, check this out, Gumbo," said Pete. He showed Gumbo how to use his foot to play the big drum on the floor.

Gumbo reached out hesitantly with his foot and pressed the pedal. The drum banged. He let out a screech and banged the drum once more, then twice. He was so excited, he jumped off the stool and spun around on the floor a couple of times. Then he got back on and started thumping the drum again, playing the cymbal at the same time.

"Not bad," said Pete approvingly. "Maybe you can have a guest spot in the band, Gumbo."

"Okay, gang," said Eliza, looking at her watch. "It's almost eleven. Maybe we'd better start our meeting. Otherwise we're never going to do it. Let's take Gumbo downstairs."

"You can leave him up here with me for a while," said Pete, tossing his hair back from his forehead in that way that drove me nuts. "I kind of like him. I'll teach him how to play the drums, and I'll send him down when he gets bored."

Eliza looked at me. "Okay," I said. "You just have to watch him every second."

"No sweat," said Pete.

The four of us went downstairs to have our meeting. Eliza held the Sacred Red Sock on her lap, which meant she was president of the club for that month. The Sacred Red Sock was a relic of our first adventure, and it got passed to a new person every month. If we needed a special emergency meeting, the sock could be flown out a window to summon everyone.

"I call this meeting of the Animal Rescue Squad to order," said Eliza.

"What time is it?" asked Molly. "I need it for the minutes." Molly wrote down everything that happened at our meetings.

"Ten-fifty," said Eliza, consulting her watch. "Not that it matters."

"It matters," said Molly, writing it down in her spiral notebook.

"So," said Eliza, "maybe we should have the treasurer's report first. Abby, you're treasurer this month, right?"

"Yup," said Abby. She and I took turns being treasurer, which was a laugh, because the most money we'd ever had in the treasury was $1.58.

Abby took a look at the messy, smudgy composition book the two of us passed back and forth. "Let's see," she said. "We made $84.25 selling brownies and fudge to raise money for the animal shelter last month. We gave $84.25 to the animal shelter. That leaves us with a final grand total of...nothing."

Eliza bit her pencil thoughtfully. "Well then, I guess we don't have to spend too

41

much time talking about the treasury," she said. "Maybe we'll have some money next month to discuss."

"Yeah, let's move on," said Abby. Molly was writing furiously.

"Okay," said Eliza. "What other news do we have from the past month?"

"Nothing that everybody doesn't already know," I said. "There was that bat Abby and I found in her attic last week, but we managed to shoo it out the window."

"And there was the stray dog I picked up a couple of weeks ago," Eliza reminded us. "The owner showed up after Molly and I posted notices all over town."

"Thank goodness the owner showed up," I said. "I don't think you can fit another dog in here."

"I see by the minutes," said Molly, "that the last Passing of the Sock was on May 24. Since today is June 26, it's time for the next person to get it."

"Whose turn is it?" Eliza asked.

"Lisa's," said the efficient Molly. Eliza stood up and handed me the Sock.

"What am I supposed to do next?" I asked.

"You're supposed to ask if there's any new business," Molly explained.

"Okay. Any new business?" I asked.

Everyone looked expectantly at me.

"Yeah, I guess Gumbo is the big new business," I said. "I'm going to need a lot of help with him, but I'm not sure exactly what. It's kind of like baby-sitting for a little kid—you have to be on his case every second. I know I could at least use a lot of company."

"You got it," said Abby. "I have a tournament in two weeks, so I'm practicing a lot, but I'll put in as much time as I can."

"So will I," said Eliza.

"Me too," said Molly. "If I don't have to be alone with him."

"Speaking of Gumbo," I said, "I just realized it's kind of quiet upstairs."

Eliza yelled upstairs, "Pete! Is Gumbo up there with you?"

"No, I sent him down about ten minutes ago," he called back. "Isn't he with you?"

"No, you doofus!" she yelled.

"Gumbo!" I called. "Where are you?"

We all stopped and listened. And then we heard a loud *thunk!* from the kitchen, and then a lot of ruckus.

We ran into the kitchen, and there were Gumbo and Archie going through the garbage. They had knocked over the can together. They both looked up at us like criminals caught in the act.

"Bad dog!" yelled Eliza.

"Bad chimp!" I yelled. We raced over to grab the partners in crime and get them away from the garbage. Archie was already wolfing down the paper from a muffin, and Gumbo was inspecting a banana peel.

"Bad! Get away from there!" I yelled.

"I think this meeting of the Animal Rescue Squad," said Eliza, dragging Archie out of the kitchen by his collar, "is now over."

"What time is it?" asked Molly.

"I don't know!" Eliza said. "It doesn't matter!"

This time Molly didn't argue.

Hand Talk!

The next morning, bright and early, Eliza called me. "I had an idea," she said. "Why don't we take Gumbo down to the ocean and see if he likes it?"

Since I had already been up with him for three hours, and since I had totally run out of things to keep him amused with in my room, I thought this was a great idea. "I'll be at your house in ten minutes," I said.

"Gumbo!" I said after I hung up. "Guess what?"

He looked up from the tower of blocks he was building. I had been lucky enough to find them in the basement, along with a bunch of my other baby toys.

"We're going for a walk! We're going to the ocean!"

Of course, he had no idea what I was talking about, but he knew from my tone of voice that something good was happening. He hooted and did his little spin. He hooted even louder when he saw me take out his belt and his leash.

"Ssssh!" I said. "Don't wake *Nainai* up!" I knew my parents had left for work already, but my grandmother liked to sleep late when she could.

We left the house quietly and walked over to Eliza's. Gumbo definitely recognized her, because he squealed with delight when he saw her. He grabbed her hand and tried to pull her into her house, smacking his lips.

"I bet you just want to go in there and make trouble with Archie," Eliza said to him. "But we have something else in mind today." She held up a little yellow plastic pail and shovel that she must have found in *her* basement.

"Great!" I said.

We walked the few blocks to the ocean. Gumbo happily carried the pail and shovel. In a few minutes, we had reached the top of the cliffs, and the stairs, cut into them, that led down to the little rocky strip of beach at the bottom.

Gumbo looked down apprehensively at the beach. Then he looked at me.

"It's okay. It's going to be fun," I said.

He pulled his lips back into the scared-smile. We started down the steps, going slowly and carefully, and we had to coax him down every step of the way. Finally we arrived at the bottom.

"Look, Gumbo, the ocean!" I said. It was at low tide, so the waves weren't very intimidating. But Gumbo did not look one bit excited.

I took my sneakers off and then I rolled up my jeans, and rolled up his little overalls too. "See?" I said, leading him to the edge of the water. "It's fun to stick your feet in the waves." I waited until a little wave came toward us, and walked into it so it lapped at our feet.

Gumbo screamed and climbed right up me, until he was practically wrapped around my head. I could feel his heart beating very hard.

"I guess he doesn't like the ocean," said Eliza.

"Why don't we try going back, away from the water, and playing in the sand?" I suggested. My voice was muffled by Gumbo's arm, which was across my mouth. He was using his feet to hold onto my clothing.

As soon as he saw that we were moving away from the water, he relaxed. I put him down and he walked beside me, holding my hand tightly and glancing back at the water every second. We walked all the way back to the cliffs, as far from the water as we could go, and sat down in the sand.

"Now," I said, "here's your bucket and here's your shovel. You can put sand in the bucket with the shovel. Look—isn't that fun?" I demonstrated to him.

He looked happy again. He dug around in the sand, scooped out a big shovelful, and threw it up in the air so it landed on all of us.

"Oh, no, no!" I said. "No throwing!" I demonstrated the bucket-filling method again. Once again, he threw the sand into the air. Again, I tried to show him how to fill up the bucket, but he was obviously more inter- ested in driving me nuts than in playing with the bucket. By the time he got bored with his game, our hair was full of sand.

We stayed at the beach for a couple of hours. Gumbo finally got interested in the bucket, and made a whole line of bucket cas- tles. Then he put a little stone on top of each one. He had a lot of fun doing it, and it was fascinating and fun to watch him. He ate a banana Eliza had brought for him. She tried once again to get him into the water, but he wasn't having any of it.

Finally we figured we'd better go home. The tide was creeping up the beach, and we didn't want him to get scared. We gathered up the toys and left.

"You want to come home with me?" I asked Eliza. "It's still early, and I'd sure love some company for a while."

"Sure," she said. "I have nothing to do today."

When we got home, my grandmother was in the kitchen making herself some tea. She edged away from Gumbo when I walked into the room with him. I made sure to hold him tightly on the leash.

"Hi, *Nainai*," said Eliza, giving my grandmother a quick hug. Even though my grandmother doesn't speak any English and Eliza doesn't speak any Chinese, they have this great relationship. My grandmother's always trying to braid Eliza's frizzy hair the way she braids mine, with not much success. They think they're really funny.

"Ask Eliza if she brought me any peppermints," my grandmother directed me in Chinese. I complied.

"Not today," said Eliza. "I didn't know I was coming. I'll be sure to bring them next time." Eliza always tried to bring this special kind of peppermints that her mother kept in a

49

bowl in her office for the customers. My grandmother loved them.

I gave my grandmother the bad news, and she nodded. Then she motioned Eliza to sit down on one of the stools, and me to sit on the other. I put Gumbo on a stool between us. I wondered why she wanted us to sit down. She offered us tea. Eliza accepted, and my grandmother put a cup in front of her.

Then she sat down and told us what was on her mind. "I've been thinking," my grandmother said, "that it's time for me to learn English."

"That's great, *Nainai*," I said in Chinese. I turned to Eliza. "*Nainai*'s decided she wants to learn English," I told her.

"Terrific," Eliza agreed.

"And I want Eliza to teach me," said my grandmother. "I want to pay her. A job."

"Um—that's good," I said to her, trying to figure out why I suddenly felt uncomfortable. Then I got it. "But, *Nainai*, why don't you want *me* to teach you English? I speak English, and I live right here in the house with you. I could do it easily."

"I want a real American to teach me English. So I know it's real."

I was flabbergasted. "But, *Nainai*, I was *born* here! I'm American!"

"Not American like Eliza."

Eliza was watching this exchange in confusion. "What's she saying?" she asked me.

"Hold on," I said to her.

"I want to learn American like on TV," said my grandmother. "I want to learn from Eliza."

I threw up my hands. "Okay, *Nainai*," I said in exasperation. "Learn English from Eliza."

I turned to Eliza. "She wants to pay you to teach her English," I told her.

"Why can't *you* teach her?" Eliza asked.

I explained the problem.

"That's crazy," said Eliza.

"That's my grandma," I said. "She's a little crazy, but that's why we love her. She wants you to teach her English like on TV."

Eliza shrugged. "It's nuts," she said. "But okay."

I asked my grandmother how much she was going to pay Eliza. "Three dollars an hour," she said.

"It's a deal," said Eliza to me. "I'll split it with you if you help me translate when I get stuck."

"Deal," I said.

Eliza shook hands with me, and then she shook hands with my grandmother. My grandmother looked very happy.

"Hello," Eliza said to her. "My name is Eliza." She pointed to herself.

"Hello," said my grandmother. "Name Eliza." She pointed to herself.

Eliza sighed. "This isn't as simple as I thought," she said to me.

"Maybe you should start with names of things," I suggested.

"Good idea," she said.

Gumbo was getting bored. I could see him eyeing the sugar bowl, wondering what was inside.

"I think I better get him out of here," I said to Eliza. "Maybe I'll see if he likes TV. Call me if you need me to translate."

"Okay," said Eliza, looking slightly panic-stricken.

As I sat down on the sofa with Gumbo, I heard Eliza saying, "Spoon." "Spoon," said my grandmother.

I clicked on the television. There wasn't a heck of a lot on at noon on a Monday. A couple of soap operas, a game show, a talk show with a lot of guests who had weird parts of their bodies pierced. *Eeew*. I kept going.

Aha! *Sesame Street*. I figured Gumbo would like that, and I kind of liked it too.

There was a song about the number 12 on,

and Gumbo was immediately riveted. He climbed onto my lap and bounced along to the music. Then there were a bunch of little kids clapping their hands, and Gumbo clapped too.

"Good clapping, Gumbo!" I said.

Next came a skit that had Grover talking to Linda, the person who speaks sign language. She was teaching Grover to say some words. Grover would hold up something, and Linda would make the sign for it. First he held up a hat. "Hat," he said. Linda put her hand on top of her head and moved it up and down.

Suddenly, I noticed that Gumbo was watching in a whole different way. He was leaning forward in my lap, almost trying to get into the television set. When Linda made the sign for "hat," Gumbo made it right along with her.

"Gee," I thought to myself, "he really likes sign language."

Next, Grover held up a cup. Linda put out her left hand, palm up, and made a round cup shape to rest on it with her right hand, just like a cup on a table. Gumbo made the sign with her again.

"Unbelievable," I said out loud. "Monkey see, monkey do."

Then Grover hauled out a pair of old

sneakers and put them in front of Linda. "Shoes," he said, but she was too busy holding her nose to make the sign.

But when I looked at Gumbo's hands, he was moving his two fists in and out, side to side. Could I be seeing what I thought I was seeing? Could he possibly know the sign? I looked back at the TV. Linda had stopped holding her nose and was making the exact same sign Gumbo was making.

"Eliza!" I yelled. "Come in here! Fast!"

Eliza came running into the room, a look of terror on her face. It instantly turned to confusion when she didn't see Gumbo doing some awful thing.

"He knows sign language!" I yelped. "Look! Watch the TV and watch him!"

She watched for another minute, until the skit was over. He made all the signs right along with Linda.

"He's not just imitating," I said breathlessly. "I saw him do one *before* she did it. He knows signs! That's what he's been doing all along, making those funny hand movements! He's talking to us in sign language!"

"Holy cow," said Eliza.

Havoc

"It must have been some kind of sign language experiment that he was in," I said.

"I've read about things like that," Eliza said. "They'll teach a chimp or a gorilla to do sign language or type on a computer or something."

"I'm going to have to learn some sign language, fast," I said. "Who knows what he's been trying to tell me? I need to be able to understand him." I turned the TV off so I could think straight.

Gumbo brought the tips of his fingers together in front of him. "He's saying something!" I said. "All this time, he's been saying stuff, and I didn't even know it!"

"I bet he wants you to turn the TV on again," Eliza said.

I turned the tube back on, and Gumbo

stopped making the sign. Oscar the Grouch was in his garbage can, making a rude noise, and Gumbo made the noise right back at him. He looked very happy.

My grandmother was calling Eliza from the kitchen.

"Better get back in there, teacher," I said.

Eliza went back into the kitchen, and Gumbo and I watched *Sesame Street* for a few more minutes. Then he started to get restless, so I figured I'd see how Eliza was doing with my grandmother.

Nainai was taking some dumplings she'd made the night before out of the refrigerator. They were on a plate covered with plastic wrap, ready to be heated up for lunch. "Dumplings," Eliza was saying as *Nainai* set them on the counter. "Dumplings," repeated my grandmother.

"Let's show Lisa what we've done so far," Eliza said to my grandmother. "I've decided," she added, "that I'm just going to say everything in English, and sooner or later it will sink in."

"It hasn't sunk in in the thirty years she's been in this country," I said.

Eliza looked determined. She held up the spoon again, and pointed to it. "Spoon," said my grandmother.

"Yay, *Nainai*!" I said.

Eliza held up a cup. "Fork," said my grandmother.

"Oops," I said. "Well, I guess you can't get everything all at once."

Eliza wasn't daunted. "Cup," she said to my grandmother. Then she went over to the sink and turned on the water.

"Water," said *Nainai*.

"This is great!" I said, hugging her. "Water!"

There was a rustling sound, kind of a crinkly noise from across the kitchen—the sound of plastic wrap being ripped off a plate.

We raced across the kitchen, but we were too late. I had taken my eyes off Gumbo for half a minute, and he had scarfed down all my grandmother's dumplings.

Nainai started screaming at him. She grabbed a broom and swatted at him, and he started screaming too. He ran into the living room, headed for the tall bookcase, and scrambled up it in a flash. My grandmother was right behind him, still swatting at him with the broom.

"Gumbo! Bad chimp! Come down from there!" I yelled at him over the din. But things had gone much too far.

"He ate my dumplings! I'll wring his

neck!" my grandmother was yelling in Chinese.

Gumbo was making a lot of hand movements up there. I could only imagine what he was trying to say to us.

"*Nainai*, let me try to get him down," I tried to persuade her. "Then we can punish him." But *Nainai* wasn't listening. She kept batting at him.

Gumbo made a tremendous flying leap off the top of the bookcase and landed on the chandelier that hung in the middle of the room. The little hanging drops of glass tinkled as he swung there, and I prayed that the whole thing wouldn't fall down. My grandmother had momentarily stopped yelling to watch in horror. I could hear Eliza behind me, mumbling "I-yi-yi. I-yi-yi."

"Gumbo," I said, "come down. Come to Lisa." I put my arms out to him.

But Gumbo wasn't coming down. From his perch near the ceiling, he eyed the room to see where his next move would be. He decided on the stairs.

Swinging back and forth on the chandelier until he had some good momentum going, he finally let go and went sailing across the room to the stairway, landing with a thump halfway up. My grandmother was yelling at him again, and he was screeching back. He scrambled up the stairs and out of sight.

"You stay here with *Nainai*," I told Eliza. "I'll go up and get him."

I ran up the stairs after Gumbo. He was already out of sight. Where had he gone? I looked into the bedrooms on the second floor. "Gumbo, where are you?" I called. No response. I ran up the stairs to the third floor.

There was Gumbo, squatting on the edge of my bathroom sink. He had squeezed most of a tube of toothpaste out onto the floor and was licking some off his fingers. I ran to grab him. But just when I almost had him, he jumped down from the sink and went barreling out of the bathroom, running between my legs and down the stairs again. I lost my balance, slipped on the toothpaste, and landed on my bottom, hitting my head on the side of the sink. I stood up slowly, seeing stars.

By the time I caught up with him, rubbing my head, he was in my parents' room. I could not believe what I was seeing. Gumbo was on the treadmill my parents used for exercise. He was turning the dials and knobs, and the thing kept going faster and faster. He was going crazy trying to keep up with the machine, running along on his squat little chimp legs.

I ran into the room and turned every knob I could find on the thing. First the front of the treadmill rose up off the floor, scaring Gumbo even more. Then it finally slowed down and sank back.

"You are in big trouble, mister," I said as the treadmill came to a halt.

"He's not the only one," said a voice from the doorway. My mother! My blood froze.

"Mom! What are you doing home? I mean—"

"I know what you mean. I had a break in my schedule, so I thought I'd come home for a nice little rest." She rolled her eyes.

"Mom, I know this looks terrible—"

"It sure does."

"But, really, I can explain everything."

"I'm not sure explaining is going to help the situation very much," she said. "Your grandmother is very upset. I don't know what we ought to do."

"Things have been going really well, right up until now," I pleaded. "He just got all nervous and excited. I promise it won't happen again!"

"It might not get a chance to happen again."

"But, Mom, he's got no place else to go!"

"This may have to be Tom's problem."

"Oh, please, oh, please, Mom, just give me a little longer with him! I've almost got everything perfect! And I promise I'll get help from Eliza's mother."

"All right," said my mother. "You can have another day or so, and I'll try to keep your father from throwing Gumbo out. But things can't go on like this. If you can't get him under better control, Gumbo will have to go."

"I promise promise promise things will be better," I swore.

"We'll see. Now, take him up to your room, please. And keep him there. I'll send Eliza up."

She turned and left.

I glared down at Gumbo. He looked back up at me, obviously trying to look as much like an angel as possible. He knew he was in deep doo-doo.

"Don't you look at me like that," I said. "It won't help. You are in the largest, largest trouble."

He put his arms around my leg and hugged.

"You might have to leave, you know," I said to him. "And then who knows where you'll end up?"

He stroked my hand gently with his fingers, and then he moved his fist around in a circle over his heart.

"I know you're sorry," I said. "Sorry might just not be enough, though."

I picked him up and trudged up the stairs with him. My heart was heavy. So was Gumbo. I plopped him down on my bed and sighed. "Stay on that bed," I ordered him. "And don't you move one muscle." He knew exactly what I was talking about.

Eliza came into the room. "I think we need to call the Lisa Rescue Squad," she said. "You need to be rescued from an animal." She sat down next to Gumbo on the bed. "Nice going, buster," she said to him.

"Do you think we could call your mother?" I asked her. "Maybe she can give me some tips."

"I don't think she sees a *lot* of chimps," said Eliza. "But sure, let's give her a try."

She dialed her mother's office and handed me the phone. I got the receptionist, who passed me along to Dr. Spain.

"So," she said before I'd even started describing the problem, "gotten into lots of trouble yet?"

"Well," I said sheepishly, "some."

She sighed. "I figured you would. Now, as I said, I don't know a lot about chimp behavior. But I did remember the name of the person you can call: Dr. Elaine Ratchet. She lives in this area now, and she's a retired zoo vet. I know she knows about chimpanzees. Here's her number." She read me a number, which I scribbled on my hand, the nearest thing I could find to write on.

"Thanks so much!" I said. "I hope she can help me. Because I'm going to have to give him back if she can't."

"I'm sure that if she can help, she will."

I thanked Eliza's mother again and hung up, and then immediately dialed the number she'd given me.

The phone rang and rang on the other end. "Darn, she must not be home," I said to Eliza. But just as I was about to hang up, an out-of-breath voice said "hello."

"Hello," I said in my politest phone voice. "My name is Lisa Ho, and I was given your number by Dr. Spain. I'm hoping you can help me—"

"Hold on a second," said the woman's deep, throaty voice. "I'm just in the middle of bandaging up an owl."

I heard the phone clatter down on a table, and some little noises in the background. "She's bandaging up a bird," I whispered to Eliza.

"My mother has to do that a lot," she whispered back.

All this time, both Eliza and I had our eyes fastened on Gumbo. He was sitting quietly on the bed, picking at the tufts on the bedspread.

"Now," said Dr. Ratchet, picking up the phone again, "what can I do for you?"

"Well, I have this chimp—" I began.

"Oh, brother," she said. "Jeepers, creepers."

"It's just for a few days," I said.

"Where on earth did you get a chimp?"

"He was in an experiment. I think they were teaching him to speak sign language. He's supposed to go to a zoo in a few days, and nobody could take care of him. So I'm doing it."

"And he's running wild all over your house, right?"

"He just started today. He's been really good until now. Well, pretty good, anyhow."

"That means he's beginning to get comfortable. How old is he?"

"I think he's about two. He seems very young."

"That's good. They can be very mean-tempered when they get older."

"He just ran all over the house and swung from the chandelier and ate the dumplings and squeezed out the toothpaste and got on a treadmill," I blurted.

She chuckled. "Sounds about right. You're lucky he didn't do more. Did he bite anybody?"

"No!" I said in horror.

"Here's the thing," she said. "You absolutely have to show him who's boss. How old are you?"

"Eleven," I said.

"Hmmm. That's going to make it harder. Can you be really tough?"

"I'm learning fast."

"Good. Because as he gets more comfortable with you, he's going to test you. And you have to be extremely firm with him. Don't let him get away with anything. Anything at all. You have to keep in mind at all times that he's an animal. He's not a child. Can you do that?"

"I have to," I said. "Or I'll lose him."

"Do you speak any sign language? That might help."

"Not yet," I said. "But I'm going to learn some."

"Good," Dr. Ratchet said. "Now, here's what you have to do. Give him lots of affection, but if he steps even one tiny bit over the line, you have to nail him. Yell at him hard.

Make him stay someplace alone for a few minutes. That should get his attention."

"All right," I said. "I'll try that."

"I take it he seems healthy? Lots of energy?"

"No problem there," I said.

"Well, then, if you're really tough on him, you might just be able to stick it out for a few more days."

"Thank you so much," I said. "This was really helpful. I'm going to try hard to do what you said."

"Good. Got to get back to my owl now. Call me if you get into worse trouble."

We said good-bye and I hung up.

I turned to Gumbo. "That's it," I said. "No more Miss Nice Guy."

The Animal Rescue Squad
Snaps to It

Eliza stayed for a few more hours, and we tried to keep Gumbo as busy and as quiet as possible. We read him books; we tried teaching him to pat his head and rub his tummy at the same time (he couldn't); we took him to the bathroom. Eliza went down to the kitchen and got food for all of us, because I figured I'd better not show my face down there at dinnertime. We gave Gumbo a lot of things, to see what he could make signs for. He seemed to know all the clothing words, a lot of foods, and other words we couldn't figure out. If he even moved a muscle when he wasn't supposed to, I yelled at him.

"You know," I said to Eliza while we were all eating apples for dessert, "I've been thinking about Gumbo's future."

"Mm-hm?" said Eliza, chewing her apple.

"Maybe Gumbo's a handful," I said, "maybe he can't live in my house or anybody else's, but—"

"Where exactly is he supposed to go from here?" asked Eliza. "I forgot."

"He's supposed to go to some zoo. They're building him a special area."

She stopped chewing. "But—but he's so *complicated*. He's so *smart*!"

"And he knows all these signs," I said. "He even has a Raggedy Ann doll! If they put him in a zoo, who will he talk to? And will they let him have his doll?"

"And who'll hug him? Who'll read to him?" Eliza chimed in.

We looked at each other. "We can't let this happen," I said.

"It's time for the Squad to go to work," said Eliza.

First we called Molly. "I'm flying the Red Sock out my window tomorrow morning," I told her. "We need an emergency meeting."

"What time?" she said.

"I don't know. Ten?"

"I'll be there."

I asked her if she could stop by the library and find us a book about sign language. Libraries are her best thing.

"How come you need sign language books?" she asked. I explained.

"Wow," she said.

The next call was to Abby, who wasn't home. I left a message on her machine.

Eliza stayed a little longer, and we talked about ways we might be able to keep Gumbo out of the zoo. Then she had to go home and put potatoes in the oven for dinner.

The next morning at ten sharp, Molly rang the bell. I walked down the stairs with Gumbo in my arms. "We're meeting up in my room," I said. I'd already apologized about a hundred times to my grandmother and promised that he'd be in my room or in my arms at all times.

Eliza and Abby were coming down the street right behind Molly, so we all went upstairs together. The Red Sock was flying out my window; after everyone was there, I pulled it in.

"We have a Gumbo Emergency," I said.

"Is it like the Gumbo Emergency about Archie and the garbage?" Molly asked, handing me a stack of books on sign language.

"No, it's way worse," I said. "It's about Gumbo's future." Before I explained what the problem was, I gave Abby and Molly a little demonstration. I put a ball in front of Gumbo. "What's this, Gumbo?" I said.

He made the "ball" sign.

"Let's look in the book and see if it's right," I said. Molly flipped through the index and found the page. "There it is," she said. "Just the way he's doing it."

"Let me try something else," I said. I looked up the sign for "shirt."

"Gumbo," I asked him, "where's your—" and I made the sign.

Gumbo plucked at his shirt. Then he plucked at my shirt, and then at Abby's.

The group was really impressed. "He actually speaks sign language!" said Abby. "That's amazing!"

I told Abby and Molly that I thought he'd been in a sign language experiment. And then I told them about the zoo, and how awful it would be.

"Well, we can't let that happen," said Abby. "It's not going to happen. There has to be someplace else."

"Maybe I'll do some research on this at the library," said Molly. "I might be able to find out about some other kind of place chimps like Gumbo can go."

"That's great," said Abby. "Lisa, why don't we call your cousin Tom and ask him if

70

there's anything he can do?" Gumbo was sitting on her lap, playing with her keys.

"Good idea," I said. "You hang onto Gumbo while I go get the address book."

I flew downstairs and was back in moments with the book. I looked up his number and dialed it, figuring he'd probably be out.

"Hello?" he said groggily.

"Uh-oh, did I wake you up?" I said. "This is Lisa."

"Well, um, sort of," he said. "I was up late studying for an exam last night. What's up?"

"I'm calling about Gumbo," I said.

"Oh, no. Do you have to give him back?"

"No—not yet, anyway. It's been a little close, but I think I can keep him."

"You'll have to call the zoo and make arrangements with them," said Tom.

"That's what I want to talk to you about," I said. "I don't think Gumbo should be going to the zoo."

"What?"

"He shouldn't be going to the zoo. Do you know what that experiment was about?"

"No—remember, you already asked me that."

"I know! I figured it out: sign language. He can talk. They treated him just like a little kid—he can dress himself, play with toys. You saw him. If he goes to the zoo, he'll just be a regular animal. Even if it's a good zoo and he's not in a cage all the time, he still won't have anybody to talk to. We can't let him go there."

"Lisa," said Tom, more awake now, "this is not something you or I can get involved in. It was somebody else's experiment, and he's somebody else's chimp. The arrangements have all been made. It's out of our hands. If I were you, I wouldn't get too attached to him."

"It's too late. I *am* attached to him."

"Then get *un*attached! I have to start studying again. I can't help you with this, Lisa."

"Some cousin *you* are," I said.

"Lisa, this is not my fault. Don't give me a hard time."

"Okay, okay. I'll talk to you soon."

"'Bye."

I hung up the phone in a sour mood.

"What'd he say?" Abby asked.

"He says it's out of our hands. Gumbo's going to the zoo and there's nothing we can do about it."

"That's ridiculous," said Abby. "We *are* going to do something about it."

We spent a while longer talking about how

to deal with the Gumbo Emergency, and then we decided to break up. By that time, Molly had gotten comfortable enough with Gumbo to have him on her lap.

Suddenly, Abby slapped her forehead. "I know the perfect person for us!" she said.

"You do?"

"Definitely. I can't believe I didn't think of her before."

"Who is she?"

"Annette Hoffman. She does some gymnastics coaching, that's how I know her. But her other job is teaching sign language."

"Neat," I said. "Do you think she could help us?"

"For sure. She's really nice. We should call her up and see what she says."

Abby went to the phone, looked up the number in the phone book, and dialed it. From across the room, we could hear her explaining the problem. "Chimp," she repeated. "It's a chimp."

She hung up the phone. "She says we can come over in half an hour. She's very interested in seeing what Gumbo can do. She's never seen a signing chimp before."

We all decided that we'd end the meeting, and Abby and I would take Gumbo to Annette's and report back to the group. I hitched Gumbo up to his leash and we left.

It took us the whole half hour to walk over to Annette's house, which was in a different neighborhood. Abby and I walked on the sidewalk, but we let Gumbo walk on the grass strips between the sidewalk and the street because he didn't have any shoes on. He hadn't arrived at my house with any kind of shoes, and when I'd tried to put a pair of my slippers on him, he seemed to hate the whole idea. But I was afraid the hot concrete would hurt his feet.

"Should I call her Annette or Ms. Hoffman?" I asked when we were getting close.

"You can call her Annette. Everybody does."

When we rang Annette's bell she immediately opened the door. Abby introduced her to me and then to Gumbo. I liked the way she looked, really pretty with curly brown hair and deep blue eyes.

She squatted down so she was at Gumbo's level, and looked searchingly into his face. Then she made a kind of little salute to him with her right hand. He returned it.

"Well, he can say hi," she said, smiling. "You can see in his eyes how smart he is. Come on in." She stood up. I loved her already.

As soon as we got inside, Gumbo started pulling on my shirt. "Er, can we use your bathroom?" I asked her.

"Of course," she said. "First door on your left." She pointed.

Gumbo and I went to the bathroom, and then we went back to the living room. He and I sat on the sofa, and Annette and Abby sat across from us.

"How come you know sign language?" I asked Annette curiously.

She shrugged. "I have two brothers, and they're both deaf. If I wanted to get in on the fun, I had to learn sign language."

She pulled her chair close to Gumbo and made a few signs to him. He made a couple back to her.

"Fascinating," she said. "He's not able to make them all just right, but he can get the idea across."

"What did you say?" Abby asked her.

"I asked him what his name is. He's got a special little made-up sign for his name."

"I just found out since I got him that there are signs for whole words," I said. "I thought you had to spell everything out with the alphabet."

Annette laughed. "You'd sprain your hand pretty fast if you had to do that. We're speaking American Sign Language. They have different sign languages in different countries. I'd have trouble understanding someone from England."

She made a few more signs to Gumbo, but he just furrowed his brow as if he were trying hard to understand. "Well, that didn't work," she said. "I asked him to show me the signs he knows, but that was too hard a sentence. I'm going to have to do it the other way around."

"We know he knows words for a lot of foods and clothing," I offered.

Annette went into the kitchen and came back a few minutes later with an armload of things.

The first thing she put out for Gumbo was a surprise. She unwrapped a package in white paper, and inside was a fish from the fish store. Gumbo looked at it and made a sign. "Good. Fish," said Annette. She wrapped the fish back up.

After that, she tried some keys, crayons, paper, and a carrot. He knew them all.

She looked at him for a minute, thinking. "I have an idea," she said to him. "How about this one?" She made a couple of signs to him.

He immediately leaped off the sofa, sprang into her lap, and started attacking her.

"Oh, no!" I cried, running to get him off her. "Oh, Annette, I'm sorry! No, Gumbo! Bad!"

But Annette was laughing her head off. "No, it's okay!" she gasped. "I asked him if he wanted to tickle me!"

He kept tickling her for a couple of minutes, and then when things quieted down, she asked him if he wanted her to tickle him. Of course he did, and the fun started all over again. "I'll definitely have to teach you this sign," she told me.

Annette asked Abby to run and get her a pad and pencil from next to the phone, and Annette started making a list of the words Gumbo knew. In about an hour, she had a pretty long list. It was fun watching her work with him.

Out of the corner of my eye, I saw a small movement. A fluffy little gray cat cautiously entered the room and sat down near the windows.

Before I could grab his leash, Gumbo was flying toward the cat. I think he just wanted to chase it and have a good time the way he had with Archie, but the cat wasn't having any of it. It let out a yowl and within about four seconds had ended up wedged in behind the sofa. It looked like it had been plugged into an electric socket. Gumbo jumped around, hooting and trying to reach in.

I grabbed him roughly, picked him up, marched him across the room, and more or less threw him onto a chair. "You bad, bad, terrible ape!" I hollered at him. "I am not happy about this at all!" I stamped my foot menacingly at him and waved my arms around. "Bad!"

"The cat will survive," said Annette. "You don't have to yell at him."

"No, I have to be really tough on him," I said. "This chimp expert I talked to said so. Otherwise he'll be uncontrollable. I'm really sorry about your cat."

Gumbo started changing positions on the sofa. "*Don't you move!*" I yelled.

He did his lint-picking thing on the chair upholstery. Then he looked up at me and did the sign he'd done after he'd gotten off the treadmill.

"He's saying he's sorry," said Annette.

"That's what I thought," I said. "I'm going to ignore him for a little while, and then I'll think about forgiving him."

"Maybe while you're ignoring him I can

teach you some of the signs he knows."

"That would be great!" I said.

We spent a little while working on signs. My head was stuffed with new information, and I knew I wasn't going to be able to remember very much of what she was teaching me, but I figured I could use the book Molly had gotten me from the library.

In a few minutes I looked over at Gumbo. He made the "sorry" sign again. "Okay," I said. "I forgive you. But stay away from that cat." I went over and gave him a hug. He hugged me back very tightly.

We worked a while longer, and finally Annette stood up. "I'm afraid I've got to go do some coaching now," she said. "This has really been fun. If you need me again, just call me."

"I will, don't worry," I said. "Thank you *sooo* much for helping us!"

"No problem," she said. "Let me know what happens with him."

I told her I would, and we left.

"Isn't she great?" Abby said on the way home.

"She's better than great," I said.

We walked back to my house, practicing all the signs we could remember from Gumbo's word list. It was fun to have a whole new way to say things. "This'll be good in school," said Abby.

"Definitely," I agreed. "Much better than passing notes."

By the time we got back to my house, Abby had to go home. Her dad was pretty strict with her; she always had to be home for meals, get to bed early, and spend a zillion hours practicing for her meets. She lived with only him, and we'd learned very early on not to ask her any questions about where her mother was. It was some kind of a mystery.

"I'll call you tomorrow, after I get home from practice," she said.

"Thanks for keeping me company today," I said. "And thanks for introducing us to Annette."

Abby hugged Gumbo and went home.

When I got into the house, I was surprised to see Eliza sitting in the living room with my grandmother. They were on the sofa, looking at a Richard Scarry book together.

"Airplane," my grandmother was saying.

"Hi!" I said. "Lesson time again?"

"Yup," said Eliza. "I figured I'd come over and wait for you and give *Nainai* a lesson. The last one didn't last very long before the, um, dumpling episode interrupted us."

My grandmother glared at Gumbo. I

picked him up and put him on my hip. "See?" I said to her in Chinese. "I'm carrying him."

"Good," she said. Then she went back to saying words from the book Eliza had brought.

The phone rang, and I went to answer it, still carrying Gumbo. It was Molly.

"Guess what?" she said. "I spent all afternoon at the library, and listen to this: There's a place in Georgia that's full of chimps and gorillas from old experiments. It's on an island. They're really nice to them there. And they can talk to each other!"

"Holy cow!" I said. "It's perfect. We have to get him in there!"

"But how?" said Molly. "He's supposed to go to the zoo in four days."

The End Is Near

The next morning at nine, after I'd fed Gumbo his breakfast, Molly and Eliza came over for the Great Gumbo Phone-a-thon. I set Gumbo up on my bed with lots of things to do, and Molly and Eliza kept watch on him. They were there to chimp-sit, and also to give me moral support and advice.

The first call I had to make was to the zoo. I had the name of a man in the primate department from the list Tom had given me.

"Hello," I said when I'd been connected to him. "My name is Lisa Ho, and I'm taking care of Gumbo, the chimp you're supposed to get in a few days."

"You're *what*?" he said.

I explained it again.

"But—correct me if I'm wrong here, but you sound like a *child*."

"Well, I'm not really a child. I'm eleven years old."

"This is incredible. What happened to the graduate student I was supposed to be in contact with? I haven't been able to get her on the phone."

"She had a bad car accident. Everything happened in a rush. That's why I ended up with him."

There was some silence on the other end while he digested this information. "You have him in your *house*?" he said finally.

"Yup," I said, feeling kind of proud of myself.

"You must be one extraordinary eleven-year-old."

"Well..." I said modestly.

"Where are you located?" he asked me. I told him. "We have to figure out how to get him from you to us," he said. "I don't suppose your parents could drive him down here?"

"How far is it from my house?" I asked him.

"I'd guess it's about six hours."

"I don't think my parents would be able to do that."

"Then, I guess we'll have to send somebody up there to collect him from you.

Is Saturday afternoon all right?"

"Well, here's the thing," I said, taking a deep breath. "I don't think he should go to your zoo."

"You *what*?"

I explained what the problem was.

"Well, my dear," he said, "that's a very nice thought, but the arrangements are all made. He'll have a good home at the zoo. You can come and see him anytime you want. He'll be able to roam outside whenever he likes. But one thing is sure—he's definitely coming here."

"What if I can find him a better place?"

He was growing impatient. He obviously thought I was totally misguided. "That's impossible. You won't find him a better place. And I've already worked all this out with Professor McClellan. He wants Gumbo to come here. Now, kindly give me your address and phone number so I can make the arrangements for the chimp to be picked up from you."

I gave him the information reluctantly. "But I'm going to keep on trying," I told him. "It's not that I have anything against your zoo or anything, it's just that Gumbo is special."

"I'm sure he is," he said.

We said good-bye and hung up.

"Now what?" said Eliza. She and Molly had picked up the gist of the conversation from my end.

"Now I think we should try and get hold of this professor," I said. "Professor McClellan."

"Do we know where he is?" Eliza asked.

"All I know is, he's teaching at a college somewhere in Oregon," I said.

"How can we find him?"

"I don't know. I guess we could call Tom's friend in the hospital," I said. "But I really don't want to. She's got all these broken bones and stuff."

"I have an idea," said Molly. "I could run over to the library and get a list of all the colleges in Oregon. Maybe we could track him down."

"Well, it's worth a try," I said.

So Eliza and I practiced our sign language on Gumbo while we waited for Molly to get back from the library. I actually got him to tickle me, just by using sign language. It was a great feeling.

When Molly came rushing back, she was waving a page she'd copied from a book, a list of all the colleges in Oregon. We all crowded around.

"Gee," I said, "there's kind of a lot."

"We might as well try the biggest one first," suggested Molly. "Look, in this column it tells you how many students there are."

I started with the biggest one and dialed the number on the paper. "Can I talk to Professor McClellan?" I asked the switchboard operator.

"Let's see," she said. "We have two. Do you know the first name?"

"I'm afraid not," I said.

"Do you know what this professor teaches? I have one in Spanish and one in psychology."

"It wouldn't be Spanish. Maybe it's psychology."

"I'll connect you."

A man answered on the third ring. "Yes?" he said. The way he said it made me feel like I'd better talk fast.

"Hello," I said. "My name is Lisa Ho." Then I explained who I was and asked him if I was speaking to the right person.

"What!" he exploded, without answering my question. "What on earth happened to Jane?"

"She's in the hospital. She had a car accident and she couldn't take care of him."

"Is she all right?"

"I think she will be. She broke a whole lot of bones."

"Good Lord," he groaned. "I should have made better arrangements. This is terrible. How old are you, young woman?"

I told him.

"Good Lord," he said again. "How in heaven's name are you taking care of Gumbo?"

"Well, I got some advice from a zoo vet. She told me I had to be really strict with him, and it's been better since I started doing that. And I got help from a sign language teacher, too. I just keep him in my room and play with him and feed him and stuff."

"We must get him to the proper place at once. I'll see if I can have the zoo pick him up early."

"That's just the thing," I said. "I don't want him to go to the zoo. He can't talk to anybody there."

"Don't be ridiculous. He's going to the zoo. He'll forget all about sign language soon. He'll become a regular chimp. He'll be very happy."

"No he won't! Dr. McClellan, can't we send him to that island in Georgia where they take chimps from experiments?"

"I tried them. They're all booked up. The zoo is the only place, believe me."

My eyes filled up with tears. I *hate* it when that happens.

"Dr. McClellan," I said, "there *has* to be a better place! There just has to be!"

"It's out of my hands," he said with finality. "The papers are signed. I'll be in touch with the zoo over the next few days and make sure the transfer goes smoothly."

There was nothing more to say. Gumbo was going to the zoo.

Desperate

On Friday night, the Animal Rescue Squad had a special good-bye dinner with Gumbo. We put up a card table in my room and set it as beautifully as we could. Eliza brought flowers to put in the center. We laid out a paper tablecloth and good dishes, and we would have lit candles except I was afraid Gumbo might knock them over and burn the house down, which would have made my parents very unhappy. Instead, we just turned the lights down low.

Molly had brought tuna casserole, her specialty. Abby had come with a big bag of fruits and vegetables, and I had provided jelly beans, which I'd discovered were Gumbo's favorite dessert. Before we started eating, we all silently held hands for a moment, even Gumbo. I think he knew something was up.

He kept bouncing in his chair as if he was waiting for something to happen.

"I'd like to propose a toast," said Abby, holding up her paper cup of grape juice. "To Gumbo, who has made our lives so much brighter. We'll miss you, Gumbo. We wish you didn't have to go."

We all touched cups, and Gumbo did, too, even though he had no idea why. There were tears streaming down my face and I couldn't talk.

As we all started dinner, I tried to get a grip on myself and get cheerful, but I just couldn't stop the tears. I couldn't eat, because there was a lump in my throat the size of an apple. Gumbo picked up on my misery; he crept into my lap and tried to brush the tears away with his thumb. Everybody kept trying to make conversation but it didn't work. All the talk just fizzled out. Our festive dinner was not very festive.

After dinner was cleaned up, everybody hugged and kissed Gumbo good-bye forever, and finally went home.

The next morning, Gumbo woke me up with his usual nose-tapping at 5:30. I was already stirring anyhow; I'd had a bad night's sleep. For half the night I'd just lain on my side in the moonlight, watching Gumbo sleeping beside me in his hammock, holding his Raggedy Ann doll. Every now and then he'd smack his lips and make small noises, as if he was having a dream. What did he dream about? I wondered. I was glad he had no idea where he was going the next day.

I snuck down the stairs with him so we didn't wake anybody up, and gave him some bananas and raisins for breakfast. As I watched him eat, I felt all cried out, dry, like an old empty gourd.

My mother came into the kitchen in her bathrobe, rubbing her eyes.

"Mom!" I said. "What are you doing up?"

"I figured you might want some company on your last morning with Gumbo," she said. She patted him on the head. "I've kind of gotten to like the little guy," she added. "Not that your father has."

"I think even *Nainai* likes him a little," I said.

"You're right. She'd never admit it, though."

She watched me move raisins around on the table. "How are you doing?" she asked me.

"Bad," I replied. "I'm doing bad."

"I know it's sad that he has to go to the zoo. I wish he didn't have to."

"Me too."

I got up and washed the dishes, keeping one eye on Gumbo to make sure he was staying put.

"Do you want me to help you pack up his stuff?" my mother asked me.

"No thanks," I said. "I think maybe I need to be alone with him for a while."

"Okay," she said. "Call me if you want company."

I gave her a hug and went upstairs with Gumbo.

In my room, I puttered around, packing Gumbo's things up as slowly as I could. Into the net bag went his toys, his board books, his Raggedy Ann. I slipped in a few of my old toys as well. I wasn't sure why I was bothering. They'd probably throw out all his stuff when he got to the zoo.

I started going around my room gathering up all his little shirts and pants to put in the suitcase. Then I sat on the edge of the bed and stared.

And then I made a decision. This chimp wasn't going to the zoo, not if I had one ounce of fight left in my body.

Gumbo was getting edgy. He was no dope. He'd seen his stuff packed up like that before, and it didn't mean anything good. He roamed around the room making little unhappy noises.

"I'll tell you what," I said to him. "Why don't we let you watch some TV? Maybe *Sesame Street* will be on. It might calm us both down." I scooped him up and carried him downstairs. Turning on the television, I settled down on the sofa with him on my lap. Maybe I could come up with some kind of plan while Gumbo was busy watching.

I channel-surfed, looking for *Sesame Street* or anything else I thought he'd like. But all I could find was a bunch of stupid cartoons, too stupid for even Gumbo to be interested in. I gave him the remote control. Maybe he'd do better than I had.

I was amazed to see that he knew exactly what buttons to push. He'd been watching me. Using the up arrow, he moved to the next channel, shook his head, and went on to the next.

Surprisingly, he stopped on Channel 7, where they were doing the local news. They were talking about a dog that had found its way back to Dormouth all the way from

Albany, New York. I guess Gumbo liked the dog, because he leaned forward and watched with great interest.

And then, suddenly, I had my idea.

I stood up and turned the TV off, disappointing Gumbo. "Come on, Gumbo," I said. "The whole world is going to find out about you today."

I took his hand and led him outside to the garage, where I started rummaging around a big pile of stuff on a shelf above the bicycles. I moved aside some rags, a tire patch kit, a helmet. There. There they were, all tangled up in a pile.

A couple of years ago, there had been a rash of bicycle thefts in Dormouth, so my dad had gone out and bought special chains and locks so that we could lock our bikes up if we left them outside somewhere. Then the thieves had been caught, and everybody, including us, went back to just leaving their bikes outside the store or the library.

But now I needed those chains. I untangled them, laid them out on the garage floor, and looked at them carefully. They would do. Yes, they were going to be fine. The chains were heavy, but not too heavy. The length was about right. The locks were combination locks, with the combinations written on stickers attached to the backs of the locks. I tried one of the locks to see if I remembered how to do it: right, then left, then right. It clicked open.

I gathered up the chains and put them into a shopping bag I found on the garage floor. Peeling off the stickers with the lock combinations, I put them into my pocket. Then I left the bag outside by the front door and went inside with Gumbo. I took him upstairs to my room and got out a piece of oak tag I had left over from a school project. With my red and blue markers, I made the best sign I could. Then I rolled it up, tucked it under my arm, and went looking for my mother.

She was on the second floor, reading a medical journal in the sunny window seat in the hallway. I tiptoed over and gave her a kiss. "I'm going out with Gumbo," I whispered. My father and grandmother hadn't gotten up yet.

"All right, honey," she said. "When are you coming back?"

"I'm not sure," I said.

"You have to be here a little later for the zoo people, right?"

"I guess so."

"Just keep an eye on the time. Don't be too long."

"I won't," I said. I was hoping that was the truth. I really didn't know how much time this would take. If things went right, maybe it wouldn't take too long. If things went wrong, my timing wouldn't matter much.

My mother gave Gumbo another pat, and he gave her a noisy kiss on the cheek. She leaned away, but she looked kind of tickled, too. I scooped him up and took him downstairs, and we left.

It was still early enough that it wasn't really hot. We walked down the street at a pretty good pace. Gumbo was toddling along on the grass strip, as usual. I had my hands full—the sign under my left arm, the heavy shopping bag with the chains in my left hand, and Gumbo holding my right hand. We had a long way to go, and it would have been easier without all this stuff.

I wasn't quite sure where I was going, but I knew the general area, and I hoped I'd recognize the place when I saw it. I knew that it was a big gray building, with the letters in the front, and that it was downtown near the big post office.

As we got closer to the downtown area, there wasn't any grass for Gumbo to walk on any more, and it was getting hotter. I picked him up and let him ride on my back. He seemed to have gotten heavier over the course of the week.

I walked past a lot of big buildings, trying to get my bearings. I didn't come to this neighborhood very often. Going up and down the unfamiliar streets, I passed the glass cube of the telephone company, and the offices of the *Courier*, Dormouth's only newspaper.

Aha. There was the post office, with its wide steps and pillars. And there, right across the street, was the place I was looking for. Channel 7. It had a huge WDBC, about as tall as me, carved right into the front of the building.

I found my mind wandering back to the first time the Animal Rescue Squad had seen those four letters up close. The letters were on the big cameras that the crew from Channel 7 had brought along to cover the story of our fight to save the animal shelter. It was then that the four of us had learned about the power of television, how one little 30-second story on the evening news could change everything.

I hitched Gumbo up more firmly on my back and walked at top speed to the building. My heart was thumping as I thought about actually doing what I had planned.

When I reached the building, I took a careful look at it. The building was set back pretty far from the street, and there was a kind of a big empty plaza in front of it. I needed to find something just right. Something very solid, not too big around—Yes! This would do. Near the front doors was a tall, round stone column, just for decoration as far as I could see, with the letters WDBC carved onto it, too.

I let Gumbo off my back and sat him down next to the column. He looked at me expectantly as I turned over the shopping bag and dumped all the chains out onto the ground. And then I surprised him.

I took the first chain, the one which weighed the least, and passed it around the back of the column behind him. Then I brought the ends around in front of his chest and fastened the lock onto them. Now Gumbo was chained to the column.

Once he realized what had happened, he started wiggling to see if he could get free of the chain. "I'm sorry, Gumbo," I said. "I'm truly sorry. But we have to do this. It's so you don't have to go to the zoo."

I picked up the other chain off the ground and did almost the same thing—passed it behind the column and threaded it behind Gumbo's back, but I fastened it together in front of *my* chest with the other lock. Now we were both chained to the column, sitting next to each other.

The last thing I did was prop the sign I'd made between us, so it could be easily read. It said, THIS IS GUMBO. HE SPEAKS SIGN LANGUAGE. HE'S SMART. HELP ME KEEP HIM OUT OF THE ZOO.

Now there was nothing to do but wait. Gumbo wiggled now and then, and then stopped for a while. It was about ten minutes to nine in the morning.

I was feeling really bad for Gumbo. He hadn't asked to be part of this demonstration. He didn't know why he was attached to a stone column with a chain. He wanted to play. Luckily, we were in the shade of the building. All I could do was try to distract him. I tried all the signs I knew on him. He looked at me as if I was crazy. I sang him "The Itsy Bitsy Spider," and then I started telling him the story of Cinderella, just so he'd hear me talking. Gumbo wasn't interested at all, though. He kept messing around with the chain.

Just when I got to where the fairy godmother appears, two people arrived, a man and a woman, on their way to work in the building. They were both carrying containers of coffee.

They almost walked right past us, but

then the woman suddenly stopped dead in her tracks. She clutched her companion's arm. "Tony! Look at this!" she exclaimed. He did a double take, just like in a cartoon.

They came closer so they could read my sign. The man squatted down beside me and Gumbo.

"Are you—all right?" the woman asked me.

"I'm fine," I said.

Meanwhile, the man made the "hi" sign to Gumbo, and Gumbo returned it. "I'll be darned," the man muttered.

"I didn't know you knew sign language," the woman said to him.

"I don't. I only know how to say 'hi.'"

"Tell us your story," said the woman to me. "We work in the newsroom."

"Great!" I cried. Then I told them the whole story of Gumbo, and what he could do, and how I'd gotten him, and what was going to happen to him. I cried when I got to the zoo part, and I wasn't faking, either.

"This is really something," said the man. "I'm going to go upstairs and get Arnie."

"Good idea," said the woman. "I'll stay here."

She stayed with me, talking about Gumbo, and in a few minutes two more people on their way into the building came, and then a group of tourists who were walking down the street looking for the bus to the beach came over to see what the fuss was, and pretty soon there was a small crowd. Gumbo was enjoying the attention, even if he was hating his chain.

"He's so cute!" cooed one of the tourists.

"He's more than cute," I responded. "He's smart as anything. He was in an experiment. They taught him to speak sign language and dress himself and feed himself and look at books, and now they want to put him in a zoo because the experiment's over."

"Why, that's terrible!" said the woman. Heads were nodding in agreement all around. Now we were getting somewhere.

The man who had left came over with another man, and also a woman in a navy blue uniform with a shield on the shoulder.

"This is Arnie Glassman," said the first man. "He's head of the news division, and—"

The woman stepped in front of him and cut him off. "I'm head of security," she said. "I'm afraid you'll have to leave. You're causing a disturbance."

Uh-oh. "I can't do that," I lied. "I can't undo the locks. And I'm not leaving until I find Gumbo a place to live, anyhow."

101

"We'll see about that," she said curtly.

The crowd began murmuring. "Let the kid stay," I heard some people say.

Now Mr. Glassman stepped in front of the security guard. "I think we've got a news story here," he said. He squatted down in front of me and made me tell him the whole thing again, in detail. I introduced him to Gumbo, and they shook hands. Then he stood up. "It's a darn good story," he said. "I'm sending a camera crew down here with a reporter. Who's free?"

"I think James Johnson's free," said the man who had brought Mr. Glassman.

"Oh, that's wonderful!" I said. "He knows me already. I'm in this club, the Animal Rescue Squad, and we were raising money to help the animal shelter, and he came to our school and did a story on us."

"I remember that," said Mr. Glassman. "Well, you and your chimp will make a great follow-up."

"I don't like this," said Ms. Security. "I don't like it at all. If you're going to override my authority, then if something goes wrong, it's going to be on your head. *You* deal with the lawsuits."

"Fine," said Mr. Glassman. He stomped back into the building, and she followed.

The crowd was growing bigger and bigger now. Gumbo wasn't so sure he was having fun anymore. He wasn't used to having so many people all up in his face. He was making unhappy noises, straining at his chain. "It's okay, Gumbo," I said. "Everything is going to be all right." I stroked his fur.

A few restless minutes later, a camera crew came rushing out of the building, followed by my old buddy James Johnson, who was hurriedly combing his hair. When he saw me, he smiled. "I remember you," he said.

"I remember you, too," I replied.

Like the others before him, he squatted in front of us, met Gumbo, and heard my story. He had a skinny little lined pad, and made furious notes as I was talking. He asked me the name of the professor and the university and the zoo. He asked me a lot of questions about Gumbo that I couldn't answer, like what kind of chimp he was and where he'd come from and exactly how old he was. He asked me to get Gumbo to demonstrate some sign language, which I did. Unfortunately, what Gumbo said, pulling against his chain, was "Ouch." I felt like a torturer. I just had to hope it was all worth it.

When Johnson was finished making his notes, he stood up for a few minutes and studied what he'd written. Then he straight-ened his tie and signaled to the crew that he was ready. They all jockeyed around, moving the crowd back, until they had a good shot of him that showed me and Gumbo too.

The camera rolled. "I'm coming to you live, in front of the offices of WDBC," he began, "where a nine-year-old girl is holding a lonely vigil this morning in an attempt to save a very special chimpanzee from going off to the zoo." I was too busy being indignant that he'd said I was nine to hear much of the rest, but I'm pretty sure he got a few other facts wrong, too. They did a close-up of Gumbo, and I got him to stop grabbing for the camera long enough to say something in sign language. They interviewed me and I tried not to sound too stupid. I felt pretty ridicu-lous with my arms pinned to my sides by the chain around my chest.

In about two minutes, the thing was done. "This is a great story," said Johnson as the cameras were packed up. "Let's see what hap-pens now. I'll be coming outside to do up-dates from time to time." He thanked me, and he and the crew went back into the building.

"Do you think Gumbo would like some-thing to drink?" asked someone in the crowd. "It's pretty hot."

"I think he'd love it," I said gratefully. I felt like a torturer again for not having thought of that myself.

The woman stepped forward and twisted open a bottle of orange juice. "Can he drink from a straw?" she asked.

"I don't know," I replied. "Give it a try."

She went over to him and offered him the juice. He took the straw in his mouth and drained the whole bottle in a few seconds flat.

"I guess he can use a straw," she said.

"Thank you very much," I said. "That was really nice of you."

Somebody else came up and offered him sections of an orange, which he was also happy to take. I realized that sooner or later, he'd have to go to the bathroom. I hadn't thought of that. I didn't have a clue how I'd manage.

I noticed there was a commotion at the back of the crowd, and I craned my neck to see what it was. I saw some signs on sticks, and then I started being able to make out a few voices. "Free the chimp!" they were chanting. "No zoo for Gumbo!" It was some kind of animal rights group, come to help out.

A young woman at the head of the group came over to me. She had short black hair that stuck out in spikes from her head, and big black boots that looked really hot. "Hi," she said. "We're the Animal Guerrillas. Maybe you've heard about us. We do a lot of work with lab animals—setting them free, I mean. We just thought we'd come out and support you."

"Thanks," I said, feeling a little over-whelmed by it all.

Suddenly I heard a familiar voice calling my name from the outskirts of the crowd. It was Eliza!

She was running across the plaza toward me, with Molly and Abby in tow. "Lisa!" she yelled again.

"Here I am!" I called back.

The crowd parted for them to come through. I had never been happier to see anybody in my whole life.

"What are you *doing*?" Eliza demanded. "You're insane, you know that?"

"Not insane, just desperate," I replied.

"Insane," Eliza repeated. "Why didn't you tell us you were planning this?"

"Because you would have said I was insane."

Gumbo, in the meanwhile, was so happy to see his pals from the Animal Rescue Squad that he could hardly stand it. He wiggled hard against his chains, trying to get over to them. I glanced at him nervously.

"Molly's mother saw you on TV," said Eliza. "She yelled for Molly, and Molly called me, and I called Abby."

"And we all ran over here," said Abby.

"I'm really glad to see you," I said. "This is hard to do alone."

There was a clanking sound beside me. I looked over at Gumbo, and discovered to my horror that he'd finally gotten his wish—he'd somehow wiggled himself loose from his chain. He started heading for Abby, and she opened her arms to hug him.

The crowd gasped. "He's loose!" somebody yelled. "He's going to attack the girl!"

Suddenly they didn't seem to think he was so cute anymore. "Somebody grab him!" called some stupid person at the front of the crowd.

A couple of the men started moving toward Gumbo with their arms out to catch him. "No, wait!" I cried. "Don't scare him!" But it was too late. Gumbo panicked. He turned and ran, and then people *really* started chasing him. He was screeching in fear now. He headed across the plaza, moving fast, knuckles to the ground, looking for cover. Several people from the crowd were on his heels. The animal rights group was right behind them, yelling and screaming at them to leave him alone.

At the side of the plaza, beside the main WDBC building, was a lower building, a garage where the news vans were kept. On top of the building was a satellite dish.

Gumbo headed straight for the garage. As he got closer, I realized what he was heading for. There was a tree right next to the building.

With a pack of people yelling behind him, he made for the tree. I had to twist around to see him. He clambered up the tree in a second, and from the highest branch he used his long arms to swing himself over onto the roof of the building. He held onto the side of the satellite dish, ducking behind it, screeching and chattering down at the crowd.

In the meantime, I was digging frantically in my pocket for the little piece of paper with the combination to my lock on it. Where was it? I checked one pocket: nothing. I checked the other. There, at the bottom, was a medium-sized hole. The combinations must have fallen out! How could I be so stupid? I was trapped in my chains, and my precious Gumbo was agitated and in danger on a roof, facing an excitable crowd.

And as if that weren't enough, out of the building came James Johnson and the camera crew, ready to do their next update.

"My God, what's going on here?" he said, looking around.

"Don't scare him, please don't scare him more," I begged. "Don't shine lights in his face or anything." Johnson nodded to me. A cameraman handed him a headphone and he had a hurried conference with somebody inside the building.

Abby bent down to talk to me. "I'm calling Annette," she said. Then, without another word, she took off, running as fast as only she could run.

For the next few minutes, everything was at a standstill. Eliza and Molly stood below Gumbo and tried to calm him down. Ms. Security came out and fussed and fumed and said "I told you so" to anybody who would listen.

The fire department came and set up a ladder and some kind of net, but the firefighters didn't dare go up there. The police came, too, but they didn't know what to do either.

While everybody waited, one of the firemen came over to me with some giant clipper things and clipped right through my chain. I thanked him and ran over to where Gumbo was. But all I could do was what everyone else was doing: watch from below and pray he didn't jump or something. Meantime, James Johnson was broadcasting the whole mess.

After a few minutes, I saw Abby and Annette in the distance. They tore across the plaza to join the rest of us. "Let her through," Abby was ordering people. "She can talk to him." The crowd stepped aside to let Annette go by.

With the cameras rolling, Annette stood next to me and looked up at Gumbo. "Poor little guy," she said softly. "He's terrified."

She made the "hi" sign, but Gumbo was too upset to make it back. I could tell he remembered her, though—he was watching her intently. He began to quiet down.

She said something in sign language, which I couldn't follow at all. "What did you say to him?" asked James Johnson.

"I told him not to be scared, that everything is going to be okay."

Johnson had another quick headphone conference with whoever was in charge inside. "We're going national with this," he said to the cameramen. A roar went up from the crowd, especially the animal rights group.

Annette tried saying something else to Gumbo. No response.

"Gumbo," I called up to him, "come down. We'll go home and have some raisins." I tried making the sign for "raisins," but I wasn't sure I was doing it right.

"Would you tell him for me?" I asked Annette.

She signed my plea to Gumbo, but he wasn't talking.

Somebody in the crowd waved a banana in the air. "Look, Gumbo! A nice banana!" he yelled. No response.

But then, a minute later, Gumbo moved closer to the edge of the roof. He was looking at Annette. He signed something to her.

She edged toward the ladder the firemen had put up on the side of the garage, and slowly started climbing it. He stayed where he was. Very slowly, trying not to alarm him, she climbed the rest of the way up and stepped onto the roof. He didn't back away from her.

There was a huge sigh of relief from the crowd.

Annette made a sign to him, and nobody had any trouble figuring out that she was asking him to come give her a hug. After a moment's hesitation, he flew into her arms.

"Ohhhh," went the crowd.

After Gumbo and Annette had hugged for a while, he sat in her lap and they began having a conversation. She said something to him, and then he said something back to her.

"What's he saying?" Johnson called up to her, his hands cupped to his mouth.

"He said, 'Gumbo scared. Help Gumbo,'" Annette translated.

"Awww," went the crowd.

There was now yet another commotion at the rear of the crowd, more people arriving.

"Let us through, please," I heard a strong voice saying. "We're from the zoo."

My stomach flipped over.

A man and a woman pushed their way through the crowd. "What in heaven's name is going on here?" the man demanded. "Where's the chimp?"

Thirty fingers pointed to the roof of the garage.

"Oh, great," he said. "Where's the girl?"

I stepped forward.

"Well, I hope you realize, young lady, that you have let this situation get entirely out of hand."

"I know," I said, my face flaming.

"Now things are going to be very diffi-
cult." He turned to the woman. "Go back to
the truck and get the tranquilizer gun, please,
Kathy," he said.

A murmur of alarm passed through the
crowd. Suddenly I felt a great wave of
strength surge through my body. For the
moment, I forgot about feeling awful for letting this whole situation develop. I still knew
what was right and what was wrong. I
stepped up to him.

"Forget it," I said. "You're not shooting
him with your gun, and you're not taking
him, either."

"We have a legal claim on him," he told
me. "I have the papers. You can't stop me
from taking him."

"Yes I can."

"You and what army?" he said.

I glanced toward the cameras, which were
recording all this. "Have you noticed," I
asked sweetly, "that all this is being broadcast
on national TV?"

He stared at the cameras. "Oh, fabulous,"
he said. "Just fabulous."

His assistant had returned with the tranquilizer gun by this time, but he put up a
hand to stop her. "Maybe we'd better wait a

few minutes and figure this out," he said. "Or we're going to have a major public relations problem on our hands."

At that moment, a man came running out of the building holding a cellular phone. I recognized him as Tony, the man who'd come along with the woman early this morning.

"I've got somebody here on the phone who wants to talk to you, Lisa," he said. "It's some kind of place on an island off Georgia."

My eyes widened as he handed me the phone. "Hello?" I said.

"Hi, Lisa. This is Dave Gibbon at the primate center," said a very deep voice with a Southern accent. "We've been watching you on television down here."

"You have?" I said.

"Yes, and we've been talking about Gumbo. We think we can find some room for him here. Things will just be a bit crowded, but we can do it."

"You can? That's great! That's *better* than great! And he'll have other chimps he can talk sign language to?"

"Absolutely."

"And he can keep his Raggedy Ann doll?"

"For sure."

"Yippee!" I screamed.

"We just have to see whether the zoo will release him."

"There's somebody here from the zoo now," I said. "Maybe you could talk to him."

He agreed, and I handed the phone to the horrible zoo man. "Yes, I see," said the zoo man, trying to have a private conversation with about a hundred people listening. "Well, I certainly think that would be the best solution for everyone at this point. I can't make the decision, though." He pulled an address book out of his shirt pocket and riffled through the pages. "Here's the zoo director's number at home. Why don't you call him and discuss it? You can call us right back."

He got off the phone, and then we all just stood there looking at each other. Meanwhile, on the roof, Annette and Gumbo were absorbed in a conversation.

"What are you two talking about now?" Johnson asked her.

"Lunch," said Annette.

The phone rang again. Tony handed it to the zoo man. He had a short conversation, and then hung up. By this time, all eyes in the plaza were focused on him.

"Well," he said to me, "you've won. The chimp is going to the island."

A roar rose from the crowd.

I felt faint from relief. I could hardly believe it was really true.

"If you can keep him overnight," said the man, "they'll come for him tomorrow and fly him down."

"I think I can do that," I said, hoping my parents would understand.

"Well," said the zoo man, "I guess we'll be going. We don't need to be here anymore."

"Thanks for stopping by," I said. I can be such a brat sometimes.

He gave me a mean look, beckoned to his assistant, and left.

As soon as they were gone, everybody loosened right up. Eliza, Molly, and Abby ran over and we had a group hug, jumping up and down all together and laughing and screaming with happiness. We completely forgot that the cameras were on us.

After a minute, we sobered up. "There's just one problem left," said Eliza.

"What's that?" I said. If there was one little, teensy problem anywhere in the neighborhood, Eliza the worrier would be sure to find it.

She pointed up at the roof. "We still have to get Gumbo down," she said.

Good-bye, Gumbo

I think maybe Gumbo picked up on the general mood down below and sensed that everything was going to be okay. At any rate, after a few minutes of sign language conversation, Annette was able to convince him to climb onto her back, and then she carefully, slowly made her way down the ladder with him.

As the crowd cheered, and James Johnson talked seriously into the cameras, Gumbo leaped out of Annette's arms and into mine. I was, of course, crying again. All the tourists were taking pictures.

I waved good-bye to the crowd and thanked everyone who had helped, including the police and firefighters, all the people from the television station, and the animal rights group. Then, hugging Gumbo tightly and followed by my friends, I took him into the

WDBC building for a bathroom stop. Annette came along too. As we were coming out of the bathroom, James Johnson and the camera crew met us in the hallway.

"Great story," said Johnson, shaking my hand. "I'm glad Gumbo's getting a good home."

"Me, too," I said. "Thanks for making it happen."

"I'll see you kids next time you make news." He laughed. The camera people all shook hands with Gumbo.

It was already the middle of the afternoon, and I was starving. I was sure Gumbo was, too. We decided to buy some food on the way home and have a picnic lunch at the playground.

Just as Annette was handing me a chicken salad sandwich, though, a strange thing happened. I started shaking. I tried to stop, but I couldn't.

"What's the matter?" asked Annette.

"I think," I said through chattering teeth, "it just hit me what I did." I squeezed Gumbo, who was sitting on my lap and eating grapes. "Gumbo could have gotten *killed*!"

"It's true," said Annette. "You took a big chance."

"Everything did turn out okay," said Abby.

"Thanks to a lot of help from you guys," I said. "But it could have turned out really differently. I lost the combinations to the locks. What if Gumbo had totally freaked out? What if we'd sat there in the hot sun all day with no food and water, and nobody had come? *I* could have killed him!"

"These are bad thoughts," said Eliza.

I wasn't shaking so hard anymore. "I'm just glad it's over," I said. "I don't think I'm going to do anything like that for a long time."

"Until the next time you do something like that," said Abby, and everybody laughed.

We finished our picnic and went home to explain the situation to my family.

My parents were waiting in the living room when we got there. They looked about as mad as I'd ever seen them. "Your aunt Penny called me," said my mother. "We just caught the end of your little drama on television."

"We let you take the chimp because we thought it might be a learning experience," said my mother. "But what have you learned? To try a really dumb stunt? To risk your neck *and* the animal's?"

I explained to them that I understood why they were mad, and they could punish me any way they wanted, but I actually had learned some stuff about biting off more than I could chew.

"Well, that's something, anyhow," said my father. Then he grounded me for a week. I didn't mind, though. I'd had enough excitement.

Annette stayed around long enough for my parents to thank her, and then she left. Molly, Eliza, and Abby hung around until dinnertime, though, and we ordered a pizza. The people from the island called during dinner to get directions. They said they had chartered a small plane and they'd be there about ten the next morning to drive Gumbo to the airport. After the call, we all talked about how Gumbo was likely to deal with flying. It was certainly going to be an adventure for him.

After dinner, Eliza went for a walk with my grandmother so they could practice English. Molly and Abby and I played tickling games in my room with Gumbo. Then we all sang him to sleep in his hammock, and turned out the light.

The next morning, I gathered up Gumbo's stuff again and got him ready for his long journey. The whole family had breakfast with us this time, and even my father was nice to him. My grandmother kept giving him Cheerios, which he lined up neatly on the table.

By a quarter to ten, there was nothing to do but sit by the front window and wait. Gumbo knew something was going on again, and he stuck to me like glue. I was pretty stuck to him, too; at that moment I was wishing he could just live with me forever. But I knew that was impossible, and I knew that this was the best solution for everybody. Gumbo would be happy on the island, and he'd be better off around other chimps instead of just people.

At ten after, a taxi pulled up and three people, two men and a woman, climbed out. I opened the door to greet them.

"So this is Gumbo the celebrity," said the first man. I knew from his voice that he must be Dave Gibbon. He shook my hand and Gumbo's. Gumbo was being shy.

They came into the house and met my parents and my grandmother. We all sat down in the living room, and Dave began talking in sign language to Gumbo, who was still clinging to me. I could only make out a few of the words: "friends," "fun," "up in the air." Gumbo was clearly interested, but he didn't sign back.

Then Dave began digging around in a bag he'd brought with him. "Gee, I know I had it in here," he said. He dug some more. "Hmmm—maybe I forgot it..." The suspense was killing Gumbo. What did Dave have in the bag? When Gumbo was thoroughly hooked, Dave brought out the surprise: a funny little bald rubber guy, shaped about like a bowling pin. When Dave squeezed it, its eyes and ears popped out in a really funny way. When he let it go, they went back in.

Gumbo *needed* that toy. He reached for it. Dave signed to him: "Come over here." Gumbo scampered out of my lap and into Dave's, and the toy was his. He kept squeezing and squeezing it, shrieking with delight.

"I think we're going to be friends," said Dave.

The taxi beeped outside, and the sound was like an electric shock.

"Time to go," said Dave. "It's probably better for Gumbo if the good-bye isn't too drawn-out." He stood up, still holding Gumbo.

Gumbo reached for me. I had to fight to keep my arms down. One of the other people with Dave was signing to Gumbo. Gumbo whimpered a bit, but didn't freak out. It was time to go.

We all walked them down the front walk, and now I was fighting tears again. But just as they were about to get into the cab, my grandmother threw her arms up. "Oh, no!" she said in Chinese. "I forgot!" She hurried back to the house as Dave and the others waited with the cab door open, and in a minute she was back with a plastic bag. In the bag were about a dozen dumplings. "For Gumbo," she said. In English.

Gumbo took the bag and signed, "Thank you," to her. Then the four of them climbed into the cab. I was afraid if I hugged or kissed him, it would mess everything up, so I just watched, my eyes brimming.

Gumbo was next to the window; my grandmother bent down till her nose was almost touching his. "Good-bye, Gumbo," she said in English.

Then Gumbo waved to us, and the taxi pulled away.

About the Authors

ELLEN WEISS and MEL FRIEDMAN are a husband-and-wife team who have written many popular books for young readers, including *The Curse of the Calico Cat*, *The Adventures of Ratman*, *The Tiny Parents*, and *The Poof Point*.

They live in New York with their daughter, Nora, and their boxer, Gracie. Over the years they have taken in many stray animals, among them dogs named Big, Little, and Archie.